peace is a four-letter word

peace is a four-letter word

Janet Nichols Lynch

Heyday Books, Berkeley, California
Great Valley Books

Heyday Books, founded in 1974, works to deepen people's understanding and appreciation of the cultural, artistic, historic, and natural resources of California and the American West. It operates under a 501(c)(3) nonprofit educational organization (Heyday Institute) and, in addition to publishing books, sponsors a wide range of programs, outreach, and events.

To help support Heyday or to learn more about us, visit our website at www.heydaybooks.com, or write to us at P.O. Box 9145, Berkeley, CA 94709.

Library of Congress Cataloging-in-Publication Data
Nichols, Janet, 1952-
Peace is a four-letter word / Janet Nichols Lynch.
p. cm.
Summary: When high school student Emily Rankin meets a radical English teacher, the popular cheerleader begins to question her own basic values, the war in Iraq, and the direction her future will take.
ISBN 1-59714-014-7 (pbk. : alk. paper)
[1. High schools--Fiction. 2. Schools--Fiction. 3. Persian Gulf War, 1991--Fiction. 4. Persian Gulf War, 1991--Protest movements--Fiction. 5. Teachers--Fiction.] I. Title.
PZ7.N5365Pea 2005
[Fic]--dc22

2005012721

Cover Photograph: Scott Squire, NonFiction Photography
Cover Design: Rebecca LeGates
Interior Design/Typesetting: Lorraine Rath
Printing and Binding: McNaughton & Gunn, Saline, MI

A special thanks to Courtney LeGates.

Orders, inquiries, and correspondence should be addressed to:
Heyday Books
P. O. Box 9145, Berkeley, CA 94709
(510) 549-3564, Fax (510) 549-1889
www.heydaybooks.com

Printed in the United States of America

10 9 8 7 6 5 4 3 2 1

For Caitlin and Sean

1

Is it too weird to say a person *happened* to me? Well, that's how I think of Connell, although this time last year I had never even heard of her. Today I am a changed person. In fact, I think of myself as two Emily Rankins: before Connell and after. Like I said—weird.

I'm sitting here all by myself in the bleachers of Sunkist Stadium. It's early, before eight, and already I can tell it's going to be another hot one. The sunbaked concrete seems to hold the heat of all the days of summer. There's a bit of a breeze making Connell's letter crackle in my hands. I got it three days ago and I've read it so many times I know it by heart. Staring at the crows, big as chickens in the field, I'm writing to Connell in my mind. I'm smart and sassy and funny—everything she wants me to be. No, everything *I* want to be. I imagine her tossing back her sunstreaked hair and laughing, her peace earrings flashing against her throat. My armpits heat up like I'm about to do a double back flip-flop in this stadium, jam-packed with thousands of fans.

Hell, what's the use? I don't care what Connell thinks. No, that's not true. I *want* to not care. Sometimes it's, like, really hard to be honest with yourself.

I haven't written one word to her yet, and I wonder if I ever will. I fold the letter and push it deep into my shorts pocket. All the cheerleaders will be showing up soon, and I sure don't want them to catch me with a letter from Connell, not after all that's happened. I try to tune in my tryout routine on the little TV in my mind, but up pops my computer screen instead, my reply to Connell ticking across it.

It was wrong of you to expect me to...

It really hurts me when I think of...

Don't misunderstand. I'm grateful to you for helping me see ..

God, I'm sick of it! Will I ever be able to figure it all out?

***

It all started last year, in August of 1990, the first day of my junior year at Orange Valley High in Visalia, California. Visalia isn't really small like some of the other towns in the San Joaquin Valley, but it has that small-town feel. I had known many of the kids sitting in my AP US History class since Kindergarten. The new person was the teacher, a tall, thin woman looking all business-like in a beige linen suit, French braid, and nearly invisible wire-rimmed glasses. She scrawled on the board in large, loopy cursive, sloppy as a man's: Dr. Connell McKenzie.

"Are you sure you got the right place, Doc?" Carlos Marquez yelled out from his usual seat in the back of the classroom. "Kaweah Delta is down the street."

Everyone cracked up. The vertical crease on Connell's brow deepened. She hadn't even been in town long enough to know the name of the hospital.

When she handed out the course syllabus, someone complained, "You think this is college?"

"Duh, it's Advanced Placement," came a voice from the back.

AP is kind of a joke. Of the forty kids crammed in the room, only about five would pass the test to receive college credit. I was determined to be one of them.

Connell flung off her glasses and hooked them over the neckline of her blouse above her high, small bust. I glanced down at mine, too big and too low for my small frame. When I did serious gymnastics, I felt so ridiculous bouncing around that it almost took all the fun out of it.

Connell held the syllabus close to her face, her reading interspersed with comments: "James M. McPherson's very famous *Battle Cry of Freedom: The Civil War Era* and Eric Foner's *Reconstruction: America's Unfinished Revolution* will give us a good view of—"

"Whoa, five books!" said Scott Lockhart—my Scottie, sitting in front, right next to me. Braces in middle school really paid off, and his quick, broad smile is white and even. He's got one droopy eyelid—some nerve damage due to an accident as a kid—that makes him look laid-back even when he's not. "I haven't read five books my whole life."

I laughed along with the rest of the kids, mostly out of surprise. Scott hardly ever said anything in class. Some teachers think he's as lazy as his eyelid, but he's good at what he likes—math, cars, and especially basketball. He's our star center, scoring his thousandth point last season as a sophomore.

"You can purchase these books at the bookstore," said Connell.

"What? Buy books? You can't make us buy books," said Roger Dobbs. His mom is on the school board so he's up on all the rules. "It's, like, against the law for us to buy stuff for a public education."

Connell put on her glasses and stared at us like we were green men from outer space. "Well, I can put them on reserve in the library, but I'm sure you'll want your own copies to annotate. Now, we'll also be doing the novel *Andersonville* by MacKinlay Kantor and Walt Whitman's *Drum-taps.* Historians can't delve into the depths of human emotion like the poets can. I don't want you to just know a few facts about the Civil War, I want you to feel it."

I got it right then, that first little tingle that streaked up my arms and made me shiver. *The depths of human emotion*—I wrote that down in my notebook word for word.

Usually not much happens the first day of class, but Connell immediately launched into a concentrated review of the events leading up to the war. She ended with, "We'll also take some time to discuss current events, history at its making, and its impact on society and our personal lives."

I knew the bell had rung and all the other kids were bolting for the door, but I kept writing. I wanted to go up to this amazing new teacher and say something—kiss-ass as it sounds—to let her know some of us wanted to learn. But then Scott's hand flopped onto my shoulder. "Come on, Emily. Hurry it up."

I stuffed my notebook into my backpack as Scott pulled me to my feet.

"Hey, babe, let's drive out to Rocky Hill after school." It was our special spot in all the valley, but we usually only went there on weekends.

"Isn't it too hot?" I was gazing at the arc of Connell's profile bent over the World News section of the *Los Angeles Times,* the vertical crease deepening on her brow, her lips a straight, tight line.

Scott's mouth was so close to my ear I could feel his words. "Just come on. I've got something to show you." He hooked his finger through my belt loop and guided me between the rows of desks. I turned to get one last glimpse of Connell, but Scott's towering shoulder blocked my view.

***

After school when my friends and I were walking to the parking lot, Lindsay started whining. "She's all into teaching college or something."

"She does sound like a college professor," said Skylar. "Not from around here." Nearly all of our teachers had graduated from Fresno State.

"She should go back where she came from," said Lindsay. "No one's going to read all that crap." Lindsay and I had been friends since the age of four, when we lived across the street from each other, before my parents built on the ranch. She had gone through the GATE—Gifted And Talented Education—program with me at Royal Oaks Elementary, but her grades don't show it. I think she got "identified" in Kindergarten because she's such a motormouth and that made her sound intelligent back then.

"Emily will probably do all the reading," said Skylar.

Scott tugged a strand of my straight, brown hair. "School girl."

Lindsay squeezed between Scott and me and linked her arm in his. "Come on, Skylar, he's our boyfriend now."

Skylar took his other arm. "Yeah, he's taking us to the mall."

I had to laugh. I'd been with Scott since February, and by now he was one of our group.

Lindsay let out her signature joyous whoop, "Waaugh!" When we were little and she erupted like that from the backseat of the car, my mom would nearly drive off the road.

We all piled into Scott's metallic blue '68 Mustang, which he loves almost as much as he loved me, and headed down Mooney.

At the Visalia Mall, Lindsay turned toward the pet store. "I want to see the puppies."

Scott groaned. "Let's *not* see the puppies," but Lindsay and Skylar had already run ahead of us, so I pulled him along by the hand. From a distance we could see there was a guy cleaning out the display window that held a hyper dalmatian puppy nearly too big for the space. The man had a familiar-looking receding hairline and a thinning, silver-blonde ponytail. His head jerked up.

"Hey, it's Gary!" I said. Scott doesn't call him "uncle," and when I asked him about it once he said Gary seems more like an older brother—way older. He lives in a makeshift studio apartment over the Lockharts' garage. "I thought you said he got a job with the post office."

"That was two weeks ago."

I started toward the store entrance and when I felt Scott resist I pulled my hand out of his and kept walking. Lindsay let out a whoop and she and Skylar darted off. Scott plodded along behind me.

Inside the pet store I smelled feral, furry mice and hamsters and heard parrots and cockatoos squawking in different keys.

"Hi, Gary," I said. "I didn't know you worked here."

He backed his head out of the display case and stared at me blankly. In fifth grade I did this science experiment where I heated up marbles in an iron skillet, then dumped them in a sink full of ice water. That's what Gary's light blue eyes remind me of—cracked marbles. It seemed like he wasn't going to answer me, but then he said, "Animals are a lot better than people."

The dalmatian puppy placed his forepaws on Gary's shoulder and yelped.

"Oh, he's so cute!" I said. "Don't you just love dogs?"

"Not to eat. I hope to God I never have to eat another one."

The shock was like a wave of static electricity and I winced. I felt Scott gathering the back of my polo in his fist, pulling me backward. "Well, we gotta go now, Gar. Later, man."

Outside the store, I sucked in a breath of air and blew it out. "Oh, Scottie! What do you say to something like that?"

"I tried to stop you."

"He saw us. Are we supposed to just ignore him?"

"Yeah. He seems to like it that way."

"What happened at the post office?"

"We're not too sure, but it seems like the supervisor yelled at him for not sorting fast enough, so he just stopped completely. The sorter kept shooting out mail and he just let it fly. Jumped on his bicycle, rode over to Grandy's, and ordered the fried chicken special."

"Maybe it wasn't his fault this time. There must be a reason for that expression 'going postal.'"

"I think that's about post office workers shooting up the place. The shrinks say Gary is harmless."

"It's sad though," I said, looking back at the pet store. "Really sad."

We turned the corner and up ahead were Lindsay and Skylar, prying open those dumb little plastic bubbles you get out of a machine for a quarter. Skylar held up her splayed fingers to show off a lime green skull ring.

"Oh, it's gorgeous." I looked toward the bookstore. Skylar grabbed my wrist and planted both feet.

"Help me, Scottie. She's headed straight for the books."

Scott tightened his grip on my hand and braced one foot behind the other. When I started to walk, he leaned forward, pretending to lose his balance. "Oh, she's too powerful."

In the bookstore I went right to the fiction section and plucked four copies of *Andersonville* off the shelf. My friends backed away like I was trying to pass off dog poop.

"You can tell me all about it," said Scott.

"Maybe there's Cliffs Notes." Skylar would buy Cliffs Notes for *Little House on the Prairie* if there were such a thing, but still she manages mostly As and Bs. Her dad is old-country Dutch and he grounds her if she gets a C.

Lindsay rolled her big baby blues at Scott, her eyes standing out against her dark hair. "How can you stand such a bookworm? You belong with someone null and void like me." She leaned toward him and walked two fingers across his shoulders until she was draped over him. Lindsay has always been a big flirt, and it never bothered me. I figured she was just messing around, out to have a good time.

I tossed three of the *Andersonville*s back on the shelf and moved down to the poetry section. There were no *Drum-taps,* no Whitman at all, and in the history section I didn't find any of the other books on Connell's list either.

When I asked at the counter the clerk said, "McKenzie's your teacher, right? She ordered a whole truckload of books, but I doubt if we'll sell half of them." He reached under the counter and came up with the four titles I needed.

The clerk rang up the books—all paperbacks and they still cost twenty-five something. I saw what he meant. His only chance at selling many more was if some kids sent their moms.

My friends had drifted to the magazine rack, but I went over to the discount bin, stuck my bag between my ankles, and started digging through the books. There it was, the third book I touched: *Vietnam: Undeclared War and the American Conscience* by Connell McKenzie, PhD, marked down from $28.95 to $1.98. It couldn't be—not our Dr. Connell McKenzie—and yet I knew it was before I turned to the back flap and met those penetrating gray-green eyes. I began reading the "About the Author" slowly, training my eyes over each word, forcing myself not to skim: "Connell McKenzie holds a PhD in American studies from..."

"Wha'd ya find, babe? Anything good?" Scott's voice was at my back.

"Naw!" I buried Connell's book deep in the bin. I tried to turn but felt my package between my ankles and picked it up. I looked out at the glaring mall, people drifting through, mostly killing time, buying stuff they didn't need and then regretting it later. "I get sick of this place. It's depressing."

"Then let's go."

Lindsay and Skylar wanted to stay and said they'd get a ride later, so we said our goodbyes.

Driving down Mooney, Scott was more talkative than usual. I replied with a few "uh-huhs," wondering how soon I could get my hands on Connell's book. I didn't know why I couldn't bring myself to buy it in front of my friends, but I wished I had. It took me a while to notice we were heading east on Highway 198, already past Farmersville. I twisted around, surprised by my surroundings. "We're still going to Rocky Hill?"

"Sure, it's not so late." Scott turned south on Spruce, then east again on Rocky Hill. At the top of the climb, he U-turned and pulled off the road so we could gaze over the valley stretched before us, the groves of oranges, grapefruits, and lemons, orchards of olives, plums, nectarines, almonds, walnuts, and pistachios, and vineyards of table grapes and raisins all in neat rectangles of variegated green like patches on a quilt, the roads and canals running like stitches between them. And to the north of this panorama was what seemed like the brightest patch of them all—my family's citrus ranch.

I tried to scoot onto the transmission to cuddle into Scott's embrace, but my sack of new books was keeping us apart. I reached down and moved the bag next to my feet. I thought of Connell's book again, wishing it were in the bag.

Scott laughed. "Looks like you got them all."

"You know me."

"It's okay. Our kids have to get their brains from one of us."

Some part of my guts turned, low and deep, like a cat rising from a nap, stretching, then curling around to a different position. Scott took my left hand and slipped something cold around my fourth finger. I jerked my hand away from him and held it up. My chest collapsed in utter relief. It was not a diamond.

"It's beautiful."

"Happy birthday."

"Scottie, you know it's a couple months away."

"I couldn't wait. Do you really like it? Emily always reminds me of emeralds."

The emerald wasn't real, I knew, but the gold was.

"The guy, um, at the jewelry store—this dude there—called it a promise ring."

"Promise? Promise what?"

"Emily. We've talked about it before. I know you feel the same."

Lindsay, Skylar, and I used to make fun of kids who got too serious in high school. We'd say stuff like, "Ah-ha! Is that girl a lucky one in eleven?" That's supposedly the statistic on how many teenage girls in Tulare County get pregnant. They call it "the aspiration gap." A lot of kids in the valley think they have nothing better to do.

"We've got our whole lives ahead of us," I said.

"My parents have been together since middle school. Tell me, can you really imagine yourself ending up with some other guy?"

"No." It's easy to ridicule kids for falling in love, but what I found out is it's not something you plan. You find the one you want and it doesn't seem to matter if you're fifteen or thirty, you just know, and there's nothing you can do about when...

He tried to hold me tighter but I just stared out the windshield. Beyond the orchards was Visalia and then Highway 99, the spine of the state running south to Los Angeles, the big city, and north to Sacramento, where all the important decisions were made. Beyond the highway was the coastal range, then the Pacific, then Asia, Paris, London, New York, Chicago. The world was so big and I'd seen none of it, I'd done nothing. I knew Scott was hoping I'd be ecstatic, but all I could feel was let down. Marriage seemed to be the beginning of the end.

I turned the ring around on my finger and little dots of light winked back at me. I loved it and it suddenly struck me how brave and dear Scott was for giving it to me. He just couldn't wait. I thought if I took it off and handed it back to him he might even cry. I did take it off. I put it on my right hand.

"Is this okay? I don't want to attract a lot of attention, kids we don't even know talking stuff about us."

"Sure, whatever." He was disappointed, but what could I do?

We kissed for a while, but I wasn't into it and he could tell. "Are we all right? I haven't screwed up, have I?"

"No. I like the ring, Scottie, I do. I haven't even thanked you. Thank you. It's so pretty. I just don't want it to change things because I liked us the way we were."

"It sorta changes things, doesn't it? A little, in a good way, I mean."

I stared west. After a while, Scott started the car and eased down the hill. Soon we were on Avenue 400, swishing past my family's orange groves. The tree branches bent with the weight of the greenish-orange navels. It was going to be a bumper crop and my dad was thrilled.

Scott pulled into our driveway and reached for the ignition. I put my hand over his. "There's not time for you to come in. I told Mom I'd help get dinner."

"I'll help, too."

"No, really, Scott, I've got to go."

"If I don't come in your mom will think we're having a fight. Are we having a fight?"

"Isn't it just the opposite?" I held up the little green ring in the late afternoon sun.

"Well, you don't seem too excited about it. In fact, you've been acting sort of distant ever since we left the bookstore. Are you mad about all the teasing?"

"Of course not." I kissed him quick and neat in case my little brother was spying on us through the window, then dashed in through the garage and dumped my stuff on the kitchen table. Ryan was at the counter piling peanut butter on celery.

"Where's Mom?"

Ryan didn't look up, concentrating on sticking raisins into the peanut butter—bugs on a log.

I waited a beat and then yelled, "Ryan!"

"At the packinghouse."

I ran out the door, out the back gate, and through the orange groves. Our packinghouse is two miles away by car, but only a half mile the way the crow flies. When I reached the office, I burst through the door and leaned on the counter to catch my breath.

Mom looked up from the computer monitor. "Oh, hi, hon. Where's Scott? You guys have a fight?"

"No. We've been hanging out at the mall and stuff. We saw Gary. He's working at the pet store now. Can I borrow the car?"

"Where to, Emmie-Em?"

"The mall."

My mom just shook her head and peered back at the monitor. "I thought Gary got on at the post office."

"We've got this new history teacher, Dr. McKenzie, and she's going to be super hard. She spent the whole period talking about history—just straight history and all the required reading, not the cute things her cat does or her trip to Alaska or...We're doing *Andersonville*."

Mom scrunched her face. "Ugh, how grisly."

"It is? You'll still read it with me, won't you?" My mom had done all my required reading with me since *Charlotte's Web*. "Can I borrow the keys?"

"You know we're trying to cut out all these unnecessary trips into town. It's twenty miles round-trip and wear and tear on the car. Get the book tomorrow after school."

"Then can I take the pickup?"

"You haven't heard a word I've said."

"I have to read this one book tonight." I ran around the counter, took the pickup keys off the hook, and dangled them in the air, bouncing on the balls of my feet. "Please?"

This time when Mom shook her head she was smiling. "Wear your seat belt."

"I always do."

I ran to the house, got my purse, and leaped into the pickup. I backed out of our drive and drove west on Avenue 400. I'm sure I had a goofy grin on my face, thinking about holding Connell's book. I braked at the stop sign at the intersection of Highway 63 and locked eyes with Scott. He was parked there, leaning out his window and talking to Jose Morales, a guard on the basketball team and the son of our ranch manager. A flash of heat rose up my neck into my face. I wiggled my fingers at him, then made the turn. I could tell him my mom sent me to the Circle K for some milk or some other phony alibi, but nothing could erase the betrayed look on Scott's face. I already felt he had caught me in a lie. I checked the rearview mirror for his Mustang, knowing it wouldn't be there. Scott would never follow me around to see what I was up to, but a guilty conscience made me paranoid.

At the mall I managed to pay for Connell's book and run out to the truck before opening up to the flap copy. Big, important words jumped out at me: Vassar, Harvard, Fulbright, Guggenheim.

Driving home I resolved to read the whole book, cover to cover. I fantasized talking to Connell one day after class and nonchalantly dropping a reference to her book. The surprised, happy look she would give me—I played it over and over in my mind, my face warming to a glow. A chicken darted onto the highway with a little Hispanic boy chasing it. I was able to brake in plenty of time, but still my fingers tingled and I gripped the steering wheel tighter. My euphoria dissolved into shame. How could I get so worked up over a history teacher and her stupid book that I found in the discount bin? I turned the radio up real loud and sang along so I wouldn't have to listen to my stupid thoughts anymore.

***

That night in bed, I tried reading Connell's book. The first sentence was about a paragraph long. I got lost halfway through and had to start over. I managed to read three pages before giving up. I turned out the light, thinking maybe I had to already know a lot about the Vietnam War to understand it. Or maybe Connell was so brilliant I wouldn't be able to understand her book at all. Maybe I couldn't ace her class. What was she doing in Visalia anyway?

2

It was a Friday in November, the weather had finally cooled down, and we were at an afternoon cheerleading practice. From my vantage point on top of Skylar's shoulders, I could see all the other pairs on the squad working on interlocking pieces that would eventually come together in our seven-woman pyramid.

"Ow, Emily! You're standing on my hair!" Skylar tried to pull her long, white-blonde hair out from under my feet, causing me to sway.

"I'm standing right where I'm supposed to. Wear it up if you don't want it stepped on." But I knew she wouldn't. Guys are crazy for long, flowing locks. Skylar was single then, and although she isn't the type to go looking, she wanted guys to see something they liked. Personally, I think long hair is a pain, so I keep mine short and sleek.

I clasped Skylar's hands, slid my right foot down to her cocked right thigh, and leaped to the ground. "It's not so easy. You try being a mounter."

"Oh, right."

Skylar would always be a base, just like I would always be a mounter. It suddenly struck me how unfair it is that we are forever cast into set roles because of our body types. "No, I mean it." I lunged my right thigh and held out my hands. "Come on, Skylar, upsy daisy."

She arched a thin eyebrow and raised one side of her mouth, a look that means the birth of mischief in her mind. She circled around, clasped my hands, and planted her right foot on my thigh. "You sure? I could crush you like a cockroach." She heaved up and placed her left foot on my left shoulder, then hesitated.

My God, she was heavy—by the looks of her I had no idea! My cocked knee started to shake. "Move the other foot!"

"I...can't." She was stuck, her sprawled legs quivering. She suppressed a laugh and snorted. It was loud and sounded like a hog at the trough. She started shaking with internal giggles. My bent leg collapsed inward, and we both went reeling sideways. We rolled around on the grass, holding our aching guts. Skylar was lots of fun like that. She had gone to Green Acres Middle School, same as Lindsay and me, but back then she ran around with a different group. With her white-blonde hair and designer clothes, I used to think she was a snob. Her family is loaded—Vanderman Dairy is one of the biggest operations in Tulare "Cow"nty. But when Coach paired us up as freshman, Skylar started going around with our group, and we've been pretty close ever since.

Coach Metz blew her whistle. She's short with a watermelon stomach and her skin has that baked, wrinkled look from too many days of teaching PE in the sun. "Rankin! Vanderman! You going to be ready to put this pyramid together by next week?"

I'd never actually done anything to tick Coach off, but I got the idea she didn't like me much. Lindsay was always mouthing off and Skylar rarely got serious, so I figured I was disliked by association. I wished practices could be more relaxed, but still they were fun. I'm competitive, but Coach is supercompetitive. In 1989 our squad ranked first in the Southern California Division of the AACC—American Association of Competitive Cheerleaders—which included a lot of hotshot high schools in LA. The pyramid was our most challenging move yet, and my six years of gymnastics put me at the top of the structure. I was supposed to launch off the mini-tramp into a flip, catapult into a handspring, land in a reverse thigh stand on Sharon, climb onto Lindsay's and Donna's backs, step onto Skylar's lunged thigh, and end up in a shoulder stand fourteen feet above the ground. I held that position three long seconds, then flipped into the arms of two waiting teammates. Pacing was everything—the girls beneath me had to hold their positions a lot longer. Five seconds too long and things got shaky, eight seconds too long and the pyramid crumbled into a pile of angry, writhing, embarrassed teammates.

By the end of practice I was moving up and down Skylar's body like it was a ladder.

Coach blew her whistle and gave us some final instructions. Lindsay joined Skylar and I as we started toward the locker room. "I can't believe you're not having a Sweet Sixteen party, Emily."

"She's having one," said Skylar. "She just didn't invite us."

"We sure had a blast last year, TPing Carlos's and running wild at all hours of the night."

"We're getting a little old for TPing," I said.

"Never too old to run wild," said Skylar.

I laughed, thinking the stricter the parents the wilder the kid. "Mom will have a cake at dinner tomorrow night and some presents, of course, and then Scott's taking me to a movie."

"Sounds anticlimactic," said Lindsay. "How about if we pick you up later and we have a girls' night out?"

"Can't. I gotta study for our history midterm."

"Oh, don't study," said Lindsay. "If you flunk with the rest of us, then McKenzie will just have to lower her standards."

"It won't be that bad," I said, even though I had planned to study every minute of the weekend.

"Well, then, here." Lindsay stuck a card in my hand. When I took it out of the envelope I saw a goose on the front with a blue ribbon around its neck. It was one of those cards that is blank inside, and Lindsay had written "Happy Birthday" and included a gift certificate to the mall.

"Gee, thanks," I said, "but I don't get it exactly. The goose, I mean."

"Oh," said Lindsay. "I thought she looked just like you. I mean, see her eyes? They're looking straight ahead like she knows exactly where she's going."

"Let me see," said Skylar, grabbing the card from me. "Oh, yeah! She does act like she knows what she's doing."

At first I thought the card was some joke, but then I was kind of flattered. I didn't know this is what my friends thought of me. Somehow they had gotten the idea I knew where I was headed in life. I only wished I felt the same about myself.

***

Saturday night Scott and I had been parked in the southwest grove of my family's ranch for sometime. My lips felt puffy with kissing. The windows of the Mustang were steamed up.

Scott's mouth was warm against my ear, his voice low and soft. "Let's move into the back."

My body felt so relaxed it could have poured like liquid between the bucket seats. "It's too hard to stop there."

"Let's not stop this time."

I could see Lindsay's pretty mouth, gaping with derisive laughter: a lucky one in eleven. My voice seemed distant, like it wasn't me talking. "I don't know if I could go through an abortion."

"What?!" Scott bolted upright, jolting me out of the warm scoop of his arms.

"Well, sometimes I think what if it is a human life with a soul and everything and then other times I think a fertilized egg is not much different than an unfertilized one getting swept out of my body with every period. I used to worry Carlos's dad might turn up as the anesthesiologist and then word would get around, but then I found out just the pregnancy test is done in Visalia and the abortions in Fresno. No one would ever know. It's only three hundred dollars—cash. That's not so much. It takes about three hours, but after they don't let you drive so you have to have someone drive you home, but then I guess you'd be there for me, right?"

Scott was staring out the windshield, his lips forming silent words. "You've been through this with someone."

"No, I haven't."

"It was Lindsay, right?"

"Lindsay! Why would it be Lindsay?"

"I've heard stuff."

"Well, shame on you for listening. It was Carlos, I'll bet. He should keep his mouth shut about—"

"All right, then—Sharon. If a girl messes around enough, especially when she's drunk...I didn't know you were that close to Sharon."

I gripped his hard bicep and shook him. "Will you listen? I just looked in the yellow pages under 'A' for abortion and made the phone call. They're happy to answer anyone's questions."

A sudden gust caused the dappled shadows of the orange trees to sweep across his stern face. "I just don't get you sometimes. Why would you ask if you didn't need to?"

"To help me decide if I wanted us to start. Isn't that what we're talking about?"

"Neither one of us is dumb enough to do it without birth control."

"Rubbers break. I'd have to ask my mom to make the doctor's appointment for pills, and even those aren't one hundred percent."

"Can't we cross that bridge when we come to it?"

"We've come to it! We're standing here one foot in the air ready to take the first step!"

"Oh, Emily, you can't control your whole life."

"I can control this. And there's other stuff to consider, too, like we've got a good thing, we're good friends. Sex might screw that up, and what about if we break up? I'd feel terrible, and every time I saw you at school or somewhere, I couldn't help but think—"

"Talk, talk, talk!" His large bony hands bounced in the air. "You talk every blessed thing into the ground."

"Sorry." I pressed the back of my hand against his cheek, the little green stone of the promise ring wedged between us. We never had discussed what "the promise" was exactly. I was afraid Scott thought it was something more meaningful than I did, which wasn't quite honest of me, but I didn't dare confront him. Mainly I wore the ring because I knew he would have been crushed if I had rejected it, and I didn't want to lose him.

After a painful moment of silence I said, "Scottie, don't be mad at me."

"I'm not mad, just frustrated."

"Come here." I pulled at the front of his shirt, moving him into the passenger's seat. I scooted onto his lap facing him. I held his head in my hands, looked into his eyes.

He scowled back at me. "Can't you ever just go for it?"

Then I did it: the bold, the outrageous. I whipped my sweater over my head and slipped off my bra and sat there tingling in the cold. His eyes nearly popped out of his head. He twisted his neck, looking all around the car as if there were people lurking in the oranges spying on us. He reached down, grabbed my sweater, and clumsily dressed me, I was surprised how quick. "You'll freeze," he said, but he was much happier then.

"Never, not in the San Joaquin Valley, not since 1937 anyway."

He shifted back to the driver's seat and I got dressed properly—my sweater frontward and right side out.

Scott drove back around to the front of my house. After we kissed goodnight he said, "It's okay with me if we wait, Emily. It's all your talk about it—that's what drives me nuts."

"That's how I am."

"I know. It gets to me, though."

We left it at that, a silence that hung as heavy as the big, round oranges ripening all around us.

Of course my mom was waiting up for me. I was really tired so I only talked to her for a few minutes, her eyes darting between my face and my ring, an annoying habit she had acquired. Naturally I hadn't been so dumb as to tell her it was a promise ring, but she's very intuitive, and besides, a boy giving a girl a ring usually means something.

Later, while I was getting ready for bed, she poked her head in my room to suggest I wear my new red plaid flannel pajama bottoms and the gray baseball jersey–style top with matching trim, which I had just gotten for my birthday. I clumsily ripped off the tags although I'd rather have worn my comfy, ratty, faded yellow p.j.s. I didn't think any more about it, but I should have.

***

"Out of that bed, girl. You're being kidnapped." The voice was low and snarling, but female—Skylar.

At first I thought I was dreaming. I rolled over and checked the luminous red numbers on my digital clock: 2:16. I groaned.

"We'll teach you to not have a birthday party." Lindsay pounced with both knees on my bed and started bouncing. "Come on, get up, get up."

Of course they wouldn't let me change, even though they were both wearing jeans. I just got to throw on a sweatshirt.

My mom stood at the back door in her bathrobe, arms crossed but smiling. "Only a couple of hours, girls. And give me a call. I want to know where you end up."

"We will, Mrs. Rankin," Skylar chanted in a singsong voice.

"Fat chance," Lindsay muttered so my mom couldn't hear.

It was going to be a long night.

We got into Lindsay's mom's SUV, Skylar riding shotgun and me, their captor, stuck in the back. "First we need supplies," said Lindsay.

"First we need a drink." Skylar pulled out her Little Mermaid thermos and passed it to me. It felt empty.

"Hey, there's nothing in here."

"There's something, all right," she said mysteriously.

I squinted, trying to look into the dark thermos with one eye. Then I smelled it—some kind of booze. "Oh, boy, a whole thimbleful."

"Waaaugh!" hooted Lindsay.

"Well, what do you expect? If my dad finds any of his brandy missing I'm grounded for life."

I tossed it back because that was what was expected of me. It felt hot and sharp on my tongue.

Vons grocery store is open all night, but I don't see why. There was no one in there but clerks stocking shelves. They gave us funny looks—Lindsay with her obnoxious "waaaugh," Skylar pumping the shopping cart and riding it like a scooter, and me in my pajamas. We bought soda, chips, gerkins, brownies, Red Vines, and Cheez Whiz. No toilet paper, thank God, but I should have been suspicious of the Cheez Whiz without crackers.

Back in the car, Skylar called, "Truth or dare?" I don't know why she bothered asking—they both knew I'd never choose "truth."

"I dare you to write 'I love you' in Cheez Whiz all over the Mustang."

"Why don't I just stab him in the heart instead? That stuff will take the paint off."

"We gotta do something to Scottie," said Lindsay. "I know, we'll get him a Big Mac and throw it on his porch."

It was true—Scott loved McDonald's, probably too much for his own good. "But he won't find it 'til morning," I said.

"Waaaugh!" shrieked Lindsay. Skylar laughed uproariously, beating the dashboard with her fists.

"I don't get it. It'll be all cold and soggy."

"Waaugh!" Lindsay steered into the drive-thru and ordered a Number Four. She handed the warm, heavy bag back to me. I opened it and the smell of hot, heavenly fries wafted to my nostrils. I placed one salty, crispy morsel on my tongue. Hmm, better than any of the junk we'd bought at the store. Amazing how wonderful something could be fresh and hot and how disgusting stone cold and stale.

Driving over to Scott's, Skylar slapped Lindsay on the arm and asked, "Truth or dare?"

"Truth." Lindsay nodded her head to the beat of the rock music blaring from the radio.

"Are you getting back with Carlos again?" I asked. "Because I heard—"

"Ask her something good," said Skylar. "Gimme me one of those fries. Hmm...Ask her if she's done it with him. Ask her how many times. No, how old was she when she first started—sixth grade?"

"Shut up!" Lindsay took a swing at Skylar, causing the car to swerve. "He's really changed."

Skylar turned and arched one eyebrow at me, one side of her mouth turned up. "Yeah, he's hotter now."

I laughed. Carlos and Lindsay have been on and off since middle school. They hold the record for the shortest relationship ever: one time in seventh grade they got together at break and broke up at lunch. There's something sweet about Carlos, though. He hugs his mom goodbye in front of other kids. He hugs his dad, too, and his brothers. Come to think of it, they're a hugging kind of family.

"You could *not* go with Carlos," I suggested. "It would save you the trouble of breaking up with him again."

"Who says I'm gonna be with Carlos?" Lindsay pulled up in front of Scott's house and turned off the lights and motor. That worried me a little. I thought it was going to be a simple drive-by—dump the sack of food and go. The house was dark but the driveway was flooded with a bright light streaming from Gary's apartment over the garage.

"Uh-oh. That creep is up. He'll catch us," said Lindsay.

"Oooh! Risk!" Skylar rubbed her palms together.

Caught in the glaring light, the whites of Lindsay's eyes shined. "Emily, truth or dare. I dare you to go knock on weirdo's door."

It wasn't even my turn. My voice came out flat and bored. "What for?"

"Who gives a damn? Just do it."

I jumped out of the car, ran up the drive, and took the outside stairs two at a time. I was more winded than I expected, my pulse thumping. I was about to knock, then hesitated. I still held the sack of fast food. The door swung open.

"Uh, hi, Gary." I felt myself wince, but I forced my eyes to meet his vague, cracked-marble stare. From behind him came the soft strains of "White Rabbit," which I recognized from an old Jefferson Airplane record my mom had. Smoke swirled through the air and a spicy incense mixed with the pot smell that it was supposed to cover.

"Emily. What's happening?"

I just stood there like a dumb-ass, not knowing what to say. I was a little shocked he knew my name. Of course I'm around Scott's a lot, so he'd recognize me, but I don't ever remember him actually calling me by name. "Well, uh, my friends and I are just cruising around and we thought we would leave this food on the porch for Scott."

"I think he's asleep. He wouldn't find it 'til—oh, I get it." He chuckled.

"You think it's funny?"

"Kinda sorta. If I was a kid like you—yeah."

"I think it's a waste," I said. "I saw your light on and thought you might like a snack instead." I set the warm bag in his hands.

"You're sure? Well, gee, I was getting the munchies right about now, thinking about going out for something. Here, let me give you a couple of bucks."

"Oh, no. Please. It's a gift."

"Well, thanks. I always did think you were a real righteous chick." If he was stoned, I couldn't tell it. I've heard that people who use weed regularly can act normal on it. He just stood there grinning, one shoulder rising and sort of twitching.

"There is one thing, Gary. May I use your phone?"

"Well, sure. Come on in. Sorry about the mess."

It was messy. Dirty dishes and take-out wrappings everywhere. In one corner of the room his bike was dismantled, some of its parts soaking in a dishpan. That bike was his only transportation and he loved riding it. There was something wrong with his brain that caused him to black out sometimes, so he could never get a driver's license. He had all sorts of twine and twine scraps on the sofa and carpet, a big twisting rope thing hitched to the table leg. My mom had some plant hangers made out of that stuff—macramé, she called it. It was probably soothing for him, working with his hands, tying an intricate pattern of knots to distract him from the tangled thoughts in his mind.

I called my mom and told her we were at Scott's delivering a late-night snack and that Lindsay and Skylar planned to keep me out all night. When I hung up I asked Gary, "Don't you ever sleep?"

"A little during the day sometimes. It's not as scary to wake up in the daytime."

"Oh. Well. Goodnight."

"'Night, Emily," he said, his mouth full. He swallowed hard and wiped this mouth. "Thanks again for the grub."

Outside Lindsay and Skylar were busy Cheez Whizzing Scott's bedroom window. Already they had written "Super Stud lives here" and were decorating it with hearts. When they saw me they ran to the car and we drove off.

"We were worried when you went in that guy's place," said Lindsay. "He didn't try to rape you, did he?"

"Oh, please. He's Scott's uncle for God's sake."

It was Skylar's turn for truth or dare. She choose dare, of course, even though she never needs any encouragement to act wild. Lindsay gave her the task of Cheez Whizzing a teacher's car. We drove clear out to some new, fancy apartments on Lovers Lane on the east end of town. Lindsay seemed to know exactly where she was going. She pulled up to a shiny black Mercedes.

Skylar leaped out of the car and got right to work. Lindsay stepped out to watch her. After a while I rolled the window down and asked, "Whose car is it, anyway?"

"Some bitch. Hey, that gives me an idea." Lindsay grabbed a second can of Cheez Whiz and scrawled BITCH across the back windshield. "Em, get your ass out here and help."

I slid out of the car but just stood there, stamping out the cold and looking around. "That's enough. Let's just go before we get caught."

"Hold it." Skylar drew an O on the driver's side of the windshield and put some cross marks inside it. It took me a minute to get what she was drawing—a peace sign. Like the earrings Connell wore.

"What a hypocrite," said Skylar. "She's always talking about the poor, the hungry, social injustice. How many mouths would the cost of this car feed?"

I shivered, thinking of Connell coming up behind me and grabbing me by the nape. In a few hours she'd come out to her car and discover the mess Lindsay and Skylar had made. Besides having to hassle with the cleaning, would it hurt her feelings? What if she saw us? I'd die of shame if Connell knew I was a part of this. I got back into the car and slumped in the seat.

When Lindsay and Skylar finally joined me, I asked, "Can I go home now?"

"Party pooper," said Skylar, tearing into the chips. "We're just getting started."

"Pedal to the metal," said Lindsay, heading east on Highway 198. "We're going to drive to the sun. Waaugh!"

Of course you can't drive too far east in the valley before you start climbing into the foothills of the Sierra Nevada. We ended up driving clear to Sequoia National Park, hanging out at a chilly deserted campground for a while, then getting breakfast at a place in Three Rivers. By the time Lindsay and Skylar dropped me off, the sun was just tinting the horizon orange.

Mom was drinking coffee in the kitchen when I walked in. I wondered how much sleep she'd gotten. Funny thing, I was totally exhausted but not a bit sleepy. I sat at the table and told her how we'd spent the night—most of it, anyway.

She combed my messy hair with her fingers. "I'm glad you had fun."

"It wasn't fun. It sounds fun when I'm telling it, but it wasn't. I kept wishing I was home in bed. Now I'm going to be too tired to study tomorrow—oh, God—today! Lindsay really gets on my nerves, Mom. She's changed."

"Oh, I don't know. Even when you were little and you went across the street to the Petersen's to play, you'd call me up and say, 'Do I have to come home now?' and I'd say, 'Do you want me to say you have to come home?' and you'd say, 'Uh-huh.'"

"How come I don't remember that?" I asked. "All I know is that my socks were always brown and slightly moist, and Lindsay's were white and frilly and she'd make me feel bad about it."

"And when Lindsay wanted to play baby dolls, you wanted to make mud pies. When she wanted to play Barbies, you wanted to skate. I think the only dolls you got were the ones Dottie Petersen gave you on birthdays. Oh, come to think of it, I did give you one. When Ryan was born."

"Which doll is that?"

"You left it at the hospital. A parenting book suggested I give it to you. That way you'd have a baby to take care of and I'd have a baby to take care of. But you took one look at the doll and one look at Ryan and asked why you needed a dumb doll when you had a real baby. You were only eight, but you were a big help to me."

I had been a good age to get a new baby brother. I remembered running to get diapers for Ryan and reading him *Berenstain Bears.* That made me think of other fun things I used to do like going to gymnastics practice and playing hide-and-seek in the groves at dusk. Soon I felt a tear slipping down the side of my nose. "I'm so old."

"Oh, Emmie-Em, look at you!"

"No, I mean it. I feel old. Older than Lindsay and Skylar, older than all the kids."

Mom dabbed at my face with a paper napkin and kissed the top of my head. "I just think you're an old soul. I've thought that since you were three."

When mom was in college all the kids were interested in learning about Buddhism, which taught that people were reincarnated and lived their lives over and over to get it right. "An old soul" was her way of saying I had thought a lot about life and had already figured some stuff out.

I hugged her hard and then we both went up to bed and got some sleep.

3

My mom came to my room at about three in the afternoon and asked me to go grocery shopping with her. We had all slept in and missed church, and I had been studying history since I got up. I wanted to take a break but didn't dare.

"Can't," I said.

"You've been studying all weekend. You have to get out."

It didn't feel like I'd been working all weekend, having gone out with Scott and run around all night with Lindsay and Skylar. Still, I had outlined all the reading and answered all but one of the practice essay questions. I felt fairly confident I'd do well on the midterm, but I was still bothered by what had happened the last time Connell handed out grades: I had slipped to number two in the class. Number two! I hate being number two, but what I hate even more is always having to be number one. It drove me crazy that I didn't know who number one was, and I didn't dare ask around because Lindsay and Skylar would tease me to death. I figured it was Elena Ginsberg, a girl with tiny black ringlets all over her head and round little glasses, who never raised her hand but, when called on, always delivered complete, thoughtful answers. Then there was Connell's book, *Vietnam: Undeclared War and the American Conscience,* which I was still hoping to get around to, my bookmark poking out about ten pages from the front. It was boring as hell and over my head, but I wasn't willing to admit defeat. I was thinking about that when Mom said, "Come on, you look fine as you are."

My mom thinks everyone always looks fine. She usually wears jeans, a sweatshirt, and sneakers, no makeup, her long black hair twisted into a braid. She grew up in LA the only daughter of school teachers. My grandparents were strict and placed education above everything. They sent my mom to the University of California at Berkeley in the late sixties, during all that trouble with the Vietnam War, student strikes, and drugs. With her first taste of freedom, she sort of went wild. She dropped out of school and then out of sight. My grandfather hired a private eye who found her in the Haight-Ashbury District of San Francisco living in a big Victorian with a bunch of hippies. After she got straightened out some, she transferred to UC Davis, where there was nothing to distract her from her studies but cows, bike rides, and one blue-eyed Ag-Business major in cowboy boots—my dad. I guess a stable orange grower looked pretty good to her after all she'd been through. After completing her BA in English lit she was happy to marry my Dad, move to Visalia, and settle into the quiet life of a rancher's wife.

So my mother isn't just any old hick, even though she dresses like one. She's got some gorgeous clothes and the style to look good in them when she and my dad go marketing in Seattle, New York, Chicago, Tokyo, and anywhere else they can sell our oranges.

Even though I looked "fine," I decided to change my clothes anyway. Then I decided I needed a shower. I blow-dried my hair and applied makeup, thinking it was all such a waste of studying time.

Mom was waiting for me in the car, armed with her shopping list, Vons ad, bulging coupon holder, and six canvas "Save the Earth" bags. I remembered then that she took forever to grocery shop. I was already in a bad mood because I didn't get enough sleep, but then I got to thinking about Scott and regretting the cheap display I'd made of myself.

Heading south on Highway 63, Mom said, "You're sure quiet."

I resented her for dragging me along and decided to get back at her by dropping a bomb in her lap. I leaned back against the passenger door and watched her face.

"Is that door locked?" she asked.

"Uh-huh. I'm thinking of going to bed with Scott."

Her brow tightened, terror flashing in her eyes. The car jogged sharply, a bit to the left, then right.

When she turned to me her face was smooth and calm. "Oh?"

"We had a fight about it last night."

"Is Scott pressuring you for sex?"

"He's not sure if he's ready either. I could get pregnant."

"I worry more about AIDS."

"Oh, Mom, we're both virgins."

"Last time you heard. That could change at any moment."

"I thought you liked Scott."

"He's a very sweet boy."

"I'm afraid it could change everything between us. If we broke up, I know I'd feel terrible."

"It's good you're giving this some serious thought, Emily."

"And if Scott and I stayed together—well, we're too young for that. We'd get stuck in boring Visalia forever."

"Oh, there's worse things than that, sweetie."

"What?!" I sputtered. "I wish you'd just say what you feel. What about my going away to college? What about making something of myself? You're my mother! You're supposed to want something better for me than what you've got."

Mom laughed. "Honey, you don't have anything to prove to me. I only hope you end up as happy as I am."

She turned into the shopping center. It was so depressing I could hardly stand the sight of it. I thought of the years of my life as oranges going down the conveyor belt in the packinghouse, getting dropped into the different holes: Grade A, Grade B, juice, rot, rot, rot. I wanted to be back home studying so I could get into a good university. "Thrill of the week," I said. "Going to Vons and cashing in your stupid double coupons. I'd die if I had to spend the rest of my life in this crappy town, running a crappy orange ranch."

Mom set the brake with a yank and turned on me. "No one's asking you to take over the ranch. No one's even offered it to you." I guess she was showing the signs of sleep deprivation, too.

I should have apologized right then, but I sulked instead, trailing several steps behind her as we walked to the store. In the produce section I watched an elderly couple selecting oranges. The truth is I love oranges. I love to set one white-veined section on my tongue, pierce it with my incisors, and feel the cold, sweet liquid explode in my mouth. I love to watch oranges go into other people's mouths, too. I love to watch them grow from tiny buds to fragrant snow blossoms to hard green marbles to round, ripe globes. I love the way an orange fills my hand before I snap it off the tree.

The elderly woman squeezed each orange in her purple-roped hand before gently setting it in the produce bag. After choosing several oranges she turned toward her husband, who gestured to her to get more, pointing to the sign: five pounds for a dollar. That's a lot of food for the money.

I walked up to my mom, my hands in my pockets. I was sorry for being snotty to her, and I let her know it by the way I looked into her eyes. "Mom, I...well, can I get something for you?"

She smiled. "A block of cheddar, not the reduced fat, though. Daddy won't eat it."

I got her a few other items, but most of the stuff she had to pick out for herself. By the time we reached the cereal aisle I was getting antsy. "Can't we hurry it up, Mom?"

"Hold on. The house brand of corn flakes is twenty-seven cents cheaper than Kellogg's, even with doubling the coupon. I wonder if they taste as good." She picked up both boxes and held them side by side, comparing the ingredients. I leaned my elbows over the cart handle and stared down the aisle. Another cart turned the corner and headed toward us, pushed by an attractive, thin woman dressed in wool slacks and a cashmere and leather sweater.

When I recognized her a flood of panic burned my face. I was supposed to be home, poring over *The Causes of the Civil War.* Oh, and her car! How did she react when she found it in the state we'd left it? Was she looking out her apartment window watching us? Could she possibly know I was involved? I was about to slink over to the magazine rack when recognition registered in her eyes.

"Hi, Dr. McKenzie."

She put on her glasses. "Oh. Emily. I thought you might be one of mine. It seems I can't go anywhere without running into one of you. It's one of the first things I noticed about Visalia. Everyone is always running into people they know."

"I'm, well, I'm, uh, just helping my mom with the groceries."

She was still agonizing over a twenty-seven-cent savings. While paying our company's bills, she dashed off checks in the amount of $40,000 for propane, $100,000 for pesticides. I wished Connell could be looking over her shoulder as she printed out those long lines of zeros instead of running into her in her ragged sweatshirt, clutching corn flakes. Mom looked up and I was stuck introducing them.

"Mom, this is my history teacher, Dr. McKenzie."

Mom offered her hand. "Bunny Rankin." It sounded like some stuffed animal. I wished she had used her real name, Bonita. "Emily really enjoys your class."

"And I enjoy her. Your daughter is quite a writer."

"Thank you," said Mom. "I think so myself."

"What, may I ask, did she earn on her PSATs?"

"We didn't bother with those. I'm sure they're not necessary."

"Oh, but you're mistaken. Not if we expect to get her into Ivy League."

I couldn't believe my ears. My favorite teacher had been considering which college I should attend? Obviously she hadn't seen me with Lindsay and Skylar messing up her car.

Mom didn't seem all that impressed though. She said, "I'm sure we can find someplace suitable in California. We'd like to keep her close to home."

Connell opened her mouth to argue, but my mom cut her off, which wasn't like her at all. "How do you like the valley?"

"I'm from back East, and it's quite a culture shock. No bookstores, no concerts, hardly a library. This bakery doesn't even sell sourdough."

"Oh! I'm so sorry. That must present quite a hardship for you." Sweet, nice-to-everyone Bunny Rankin being sarcastic to my history teacher! Connell smiled wanly and moved on.

But then, if that wasn't enough, she came up behind us in the checkout line. At the bottom of her cart lay a neat collection of apples, leafy vegetables, yogurt, bagels, and a stack of Lean Cuisines. Ours was overflowing with various cereals, canned goods, pot roast, beer, and white bread. I felt exposed as the ordinary farm girl I was.

Mom yelled at the bagger for placing our four jugs of milk into plastic bags. "Please, save your bags for someone else. Those containers have handles."

Then the checker, Dr. McKenzie, and everyone else in line had to wait while the bagger unbagged our milk.

"Good for you," said Connell. "I've got canvas bags myself, but I always have so much on my mind I can't ever remember to bring them."

"You'd remember if you had kids," said Mom. "I just want something of the earth left for them."

Going out the door I said, "I don't believe it, Mom. You were actually rude to Dr. McKenzie."

"Was I? I'm sorry, Emily. I guess I'm a little put off by snobs. Now there's an example of what the cold, cruel world can do to you. That's an unhappy woman."

My Dr. Connell McKenzie—unhappy? I wasn't about to believe it—not yet.

4

I know it's weird but I love to take tests. It feels like a performance or a competition. I was all pumped up for this one, ready to be number one. I squirmed in my seat, my legs holding the tension of a double back flip. My fingers gripped my cool, slim pen as I anxiously waited to pour the contents of my bulging brain into neat five-paragraph essays—thesis statement, topic sentences, convincing argument. Bring on the test.

Connell just stood staring at us, her pointed chin perched on the top edge of the stack of tests. "Did anyone read the paper this morning?"

"Montana's injured again," said Carlos. "Young's going to start on Sunday."

Everyone laughed, of course, but Connell pursed her lips in annoyance. "Right, Carlos, who's starting for the Forty-niners—that's just what I was getting at." The edge of her cutting tone caused us to fall silent. She was usually pretty tolerant of Carlos's smart-ass remarks, but this day she meant business. She went to the board and flipped to the map of the Middle East. "You'll remember Iraq invaded Kuwait on August 2."

Battle of Shiloh, I thought. General Albert S. Johnson and his Confederate forces attack the Union army headed by Grant.

"What are our interests in the Persian Gulf?"

"Oil."

"Right. Lots and lots of oil. Now, about Iraq—friend or foe?"

After several beats of silence I spoke up. "More like a friend. We helped Iraq during their war with Iran."

Connell smiled upon me, looking exactly like she had in the grocery store when she'd complimented my writing ability. If I had her for a mother instead of a rancher's wife, I'd probably be setting my sights on Harvard.

"Correct, Emily. Thank you. Let's back up a minute. Nixon called the Shah of Iran 'America's policeman of the Gulf.' But in 1979 when the Ayatollah Khomeini overthrew the Shah, Iran became our enemy. During the eighties we helped Iraq against Iran. And we had a new policeman, Saddam Hussein, protecting American oil companies. Now George Bush is saying Saddam is 'another Hitler' and he's calling for 'a new world order' in which the U.S. is the policeman of the world. Hitler used that term 'new world order.' Interesting, isn't it?"

From the back there was a scraping of desk legs against the floor. I turned to see Roger Dobbs leaping out of his seat. "Are you calling our president Hitler?"

"Ah! Finally I got a rise out of one of you. Now, last Thursday, November 8, Bush called one hundred and fifty thousand American soldiers to the Persian Gulf, doubling the number of our troops there. What do you suppose he is planning? You!—tell me." She tapped three times on Scott's desktop with her fingernails. He stopped doodling my name on his binder and looked at her in a daze. Connell waved impatiently at the other students' raised hands. "I'm asking Scott."

He dropped his head and peered at me beneath his droopy eyelid. Obviously he hadn't been paying attention, but I didn't dare help him out.

"I'll give you a few more hints," said Connell, her voice strident with sarcasm. "Three hundred thousand troops, tanks, jets, rockets, bombs..."

"We're getting ready for a war?" Scott asked.

"Excellent work! Students, don't you see? It's Vietnam all over again. Did George Bush ask us if we wanted three hundred thousand troops stationed in the Persian Gulf? Did he ask Congress?"

"Do we have to know this for the test?" someone blurted out.

"Our nation may go to war," Connell enunciated as if we were in special ed. "Hundreds of thousands of people may be killed. You—" she gestured toward Scott again, "you may be killed in a war you don't even want and you're asking 'Do we have to know this?'" It wasn't Scott who had posed the question, but once Connell started picking on someone it seemed hard for her to quit.

"Stop trying to scare us, Doc," said Carlos. "There's no draft anymore."

"Not now," Connell said, "but who knows what could happen in a 'new world order'?" She tossed the tests on her desk and they fanned over the slick surface. "While our history spans a mere couple of centuries, the Islamic world is over five thousand years old. You must understand—President Bush must understand—there is no easy solution for the problems of the Middle East." She stared at us, her class—a blank wall. Her nostrils flared, her lips tightened to a thin, straight line. "I can see you have no idea what I'm talking about. Take out your notebooks. We'll begin with a brief outline of the history of the Islamic peoples."

Lively chatter and laughter erupted, backpack zippers zipped, papers shuffled. I raised my hand and spoke without waiting to be called on.

"But Dr. McKenzie, what about our midterm? Can't we start our study of Islam tomorrow?"

"The crisis in the Persian Gulf is history in the making," said Connell. "We'll postpone the exam until Friday. Included on it will be a short quiz on what we study this week."

"Friday?!" It was Elena Ginsberg. Like me, she hadn't gotten anything out of her backpack but sat there tapping her pen against her palm, still hoping for a copy of the test to come sailing her way. "We'll forget everything we know by Friday."

"I didn't know nuthin' anyway," said Lindsay.

"This class is supposed to be about American history, not the whole world," said Roger Dobbs.

Ignoring further complaints, Connell turned to the board and began filling it with her manly scrawl. My classmates bent over their notebooks, dutifully copying. I threw down my pen, crossed my arms, and stared straight ahead the rest of the period.

***

I didn't pick up my pen in history until the middle of Wednesday's class, but I had absorbed Connell's previous lectures on the Middle East and wrote them down from memory. I didn't review any of the American Civil War material, but on Friday I was amazed to discover I could write about it with ease. The new section on the Middle East was a snap—multiple choice and true/false, something Connell never gave us. The test wasn't the thrill it would have been on Monday, and I was still mad at her for postponing it. On the back of my paper I wrote:

Dear Dr. McKenzie:

I regret that this is not my best effort. If you had given the test on Monday, as you promised, I would have done much better. I realize how pertinent the crisis in the Persian Gulf is to our lives today; however, you could have given us the test on time.

How would you like it if a magazine assigned you an article to write and you worked day and night to get it in on time, and then they just rejected your work and said it wasn't important to them anymore? Well, that's how you made me feel.

I think you are a great teacher, maybe the best I ever had, but I trusted you and you let me down. I loved hearing all that stuff about the Islamic World—before I didn't know a thing about it—but still, you sorely disappointed me.

Sincerely,
Emily Rankin

p.s. Stop picking on Scott. You're always teaching us tolerance, but you act all prejudiced against him just because he's a good athlete.

***

All day Saturday and all day Sunday I agonized and agonized over that stupid note. God! If I could only get my paper back. I imagined myself sneaking into her classroom, sliding it out of her satchel, or slipping through her apartment window and stealing it off her desk while she was at Vons stocking up on Lean Cuisines. My paper would be missing from the stack, but that was better than her reading my childish rantings. How could I have ever let her know how much I cared?

On Monday Connell handed back my paper, her eyes averted. I thought it must be really bad—a B minus or worse. But at the top of my paper was written "A+ Wow, you can do better than this?" In the margin next to my note, she wrote, "Emily, I appreciate how conscientious you are, but maintain a perspective. This is only a little history test; Bush could start a war!" Next to the paragraph about her getting a magazine article rejected, she wrote, "It happens all the time! And yes, it hurts!" Her last comment made my stomach cramp: "See me after class."

When the bell rang I told Scott to go on without me. When everyone had left I approached Connell. Her honey-streaked head was bent over the notes for her next class. I had to clear my throat to get her to notice me.

"Yes, Emily, what can I do for you?"

"You asked to see me."

"Oh, yes, of course I did. I want to ask you something. I need a research assistant. Are you interested in the position?"

In a panic I thought I couldn't. I wasn't smart enough or experienced. I'd screw up everything. "I, um, I'm not sure if I have time. I'm pretty busy studying and cheerleading, and I work for my parents."

She raised one side of her upper lip. "You're a cheerleader? I never expected you to be the type. Oh, that reminds me—I'm sorry if you thought I was picking on Scott. Really, I had no idea. What sort of athlete is he?"

I could feel the heat of a blush across my throat. "Really, you don't know? Scott is the varsity basketball team's star center."

"To his credit, he doesn't swagger around like he thinks he's somebody important. I only wish he would pay more attention in class."

"Don't let that one sleepy eyelid fool you. He's more alert than he looks."

"I recall his bragging the first day about being illiterate."

"A lot of kids don't like to read. That doesn't make them dumb."

"Oh, I know, slim pickings in this town. And boys are pitifully behind girls at this age. Don't worry, a couple of them might catch up to you some day. What sort of work do you do for your parents?"

"We're ranchers. Navels and valencias."

"Oh, oranges. Do you lasso and brand them?"

She was poking fun at citrus growers' referring to themselves as ranchers rather than farmers, but I ignored it. "Mostly I sort, but I pick, too."

"Because you want to?"

"Oh, yes." How could I explain to Connell the snap of the orange off the tree, the brilliant fruit filling my canvas picking bag? "I love the outdoors. It's fun to work the harvest. I've done it ever since I was a little girl."

"How about skipping it this year and being my research assistant instead? I'll pay you better than minimum wage, and I can write you a great letter of recommendation for college."

"I'd like to, but I'm afraid I wouldn't know what to do."

"Oh, it's easy. My subject is how the popular media depicted the Vietnam War. You just have to photocopy articles from general household magazines like *Time* and *Newsweek*—periodicals you can find in any library. Sheer drudgery—I'd go blind reading the fine print in *Reader's Guide*—but you could save me a lot of time. You can choose your own hours—say ten or so a week?"

"Okay, but I was just wondering...well, you already wrote a book about Vietnam and—"

Connell gripped my arm. "Who told you that?"

"I'm reading it." The pride probably shone on my face. This was the moment I'd fantasized about.

"You found it here? On a shelf of the Tulare County Library?"

"Actually, it was at the bookstore in the mall."

"I'll be damned. You're interested in the Vietnam War?"

"Not really. I mostly bought it because you wrote it."

"Oh, well, I'm flattered." She crossed her arms and shifted back on her hips. "Tell me, what do you think of it so far?"

"I, well, we've had so much reading to do for class, I haven't gotten too far into it. Actually, it's, uh, a little beyond me."

"Ha!" Connell tossed her head back and laughed. "It's a little beyond everybody, I'm afraid. It was my doctoral dissertation. Convoluted, lofty, boring as hell. I'm surprised it got published at all. The one I'm writing now will be much better. You'll see."

The bell rang. I turned, surprised to find the seats filled with Connell's next class.

"Oh! Dr. McKenzie, I'm late! Can you write me a hall pass?"

She scrawled out a note and handed it to me. "We'll be working together now, Emily. Call me Connell."

5

On Friday, November 30, the United Nations Security Council gave Saddam Hussein until January 15 to withdraw his troops from Kuwait; if he didn't, all the nations allied with Kuwait were authorized to use military force against Iraq. Connell was hopping mad. She couldn't stand still, and did a sort of sideways pacing, two steps to the right, two to the left. "Bush has really done it this time," she told the class. "What did I tell you?"

"Ah, Doc, you can't blame old George this time," said Carlos. He yawned, slumped down in his seat, and stretched his legs across the aisle. I suddenly flashed back to him as a kindergartner. When he'd get bored he would fall out of his seat. He had more ways to fall out of his seat than any kid I knew. "The whole United Nations voted in favor, except China and Cuba and some other little country I forget the name of."

Connell had to smile. "Very good, Carlos. You read more than the sports section this morning."

"Don't get excited, Doc. Heard it on the radio on my way to school."

"You heard the news, you absorbed it, you repeated it to the class. I can't help myself, Carlos, I'm excited, I'm excited." She made pitter-patter noises with her fingertips. The whole class cracked up, but then Connell was all business again. "Twelve nations voted for the resolution, so why are there three hundred thousand American soldiers and a handful of Saudis toeing the line?"

Skylar twirled a strand of her hair. "Everyone knows America is always willing to fight for the free world. Why should any other country show up?"

Roger Dobbs raised his hand. He had the inside scoop because his father was in the Air Force, stationed in nearby Lemoore. Connell called on him and he said, "Hussein knows he's got to back down or get blown off the face of the earth."

"But I don't think he will back down," said Connell. "Remember the Islamic view of death: it's highly desirable to die in battle. It earns the soldier the highest place in the afterlife, closest to Allah."

"And they get about twenty virgins each. Don't forget the virgins."

"Yes, Carlos, thank you for sharing. Hussein expects us to back down. He says the US is not willing to lose ten thousand lives."

"We don't have to lose anybody," said Roger. "We can get the whole job done from the air. It'll be like playing a video game with live raghead targets. Pow! Pow! Pow!"

Some of the guys joined in, puffing their cheeks and erupting with explosive sounds. Connell regained order the hard way, coldly staring down each boy in turn.

"Then let's say the ancient city of Baghdad, one that has stood since 762 AD, is now rubble. Two hundred thousand Iraq women and children lay dead."

"If any civilians get hit it's because Hussein placed them in military installations," said Roger.

"The elderly, mothers, babies, grandparents—"

"You can't humanize the enemy and win," argued Roger.

"You *must* humanize them! Every one of them has the right to life."

I was counting up how old Baghdad was. One thousand years plus two hundred plus nearly thirty—all that history gone in a flash. I thought of the bombing of Dresden in World War II—its beautiful art and architecture gone forever. I imagined what it would be like if Washington, DC, downtown LA, or even Visalia lay in rubble. Then I remembered that US cities never got bombed, not since Pearl Harbor fifty years ago, although we've been in a lot of wars since then. I wondered if President Bush would be so hasty to go to war if there were some chance New York could go down in flames right after Baghdad.

Connell stared out the window, then back at us. Her voice turned calm, almost trancelike. "You know, I really thought we were coming into an age of reason. Just last year the Berlin Wall came tumbling down without a shot fired. The USSR crumbled to pieces without a world war because, eventually, rotten political systems collapse from within. When the Iraqis invaded Kuwait in August, nearly every nation placed a trade embargo on Iraq. These sanctions would have worked if given enough time, but no, just when our world is coming into an age of enlightenment, George Bush comes along and flings us back into the Middle Ages."

Roger jumped from his seat. "You can't speak about our president that way. That's anti-American! You must be a communist!"

Connell threw back her head and laughed, her peace earrings glimmering in a sliver of gray winter light, and at that moment she was beautiful. "You've got it backward, Roger. It's the communists who are forbidden to speak against their government. It's our American right to speak our minds. That's why I'm handing these out to you." Connell distributed flyers put out by the local chapter of the anti-war organization Beyond War. On it was a photograph of a soldier in a body bag stretched out on a gurney. It read:

> Stop the WAR before it happens! President Bush says he has everyone's support to take whatever action he chooses, including war. You must let him know war is not an option!

Call the White House opinion line every day and ask friends to do likewise.

Call or write our congressman, Cal Dooley. Tell him we must maintain sanctions for as long as it takes to reach a peaceful solution.

Join us every Sunday, 1-2 p.m., at the northwest corner of Mooney Boulevard and Walnut Avenue for a peaceful demonstration.

Connell said, "I hope you'll find it in your consciences to do what you can to prevent this war." She then went on to present a lecture on the reconstruction of the South.

After class Roger made a big show of ripping up his flyer and tossing it in the wastebasket. Many of the other kids copied him, including Scott and Lindsay. But that didn't stop me from arguing against the war at lunch.

"I think Dr. McKenzie is right," I said, carefully using her last name in front of my friends. I always called her Connell when I handed her another stack of photocopies of magazine articles. Once, I had slipped in front of Scott, and he'd replied in a sarcastic tone, "Oh, so it's Connell now, is it?"

"I think she made some good points, too," said Skylar. "Not going to war is always better than going to war, but Bush has made up his mind, so what can we do about it?"

"The US has to protect its interests abroad," said Scott. "We can't walk away from all that oil. We need it."

This is what I expected of my friends, but I was surprised how much it disappointed me. "So none of you guys want to go to that peace thing on Sunday?"

Lindsay rolled her eyes. "Stand out on Mooney, waving a sign and acting un-American in front of God and everybody? You're out of your ever-lovin' mind, Emmie."

"I couldn't do anything like that and you know it," said Scott. "It would be like me spitting in my own uncle's face."

"I'm sorry Gary wasn't treated with more respect when he got off the plane from Vietnam," I said. "But I'm more sorry he went at all."

"What was he supposed to do? Be a coward and run off to Canada? Disgrace his family and go to jail?"

"I'm not saying that. I'm just sorry there was that awful war and so many people suffered and died in it." I shuddered, thinking of some of the photographs I'd seen in the magazine articles I was photocopying for Connell. The one that got me the most was a little naked Vietnamese girl running and screaming in agony, napalm burning her back. "Wouldn't it be good if this time war was avoided?"

"There will always be war," said Scott.

"Especially if people go on thinking like that," I said.

"It's human nature," he said.

"It's not *my* nature."

Scott frowned. "McKenzie—she has really got to you."

Lindsay erupted with a high-pitched scream. Carlos, his black hair sticking up wild, had come up behind her and was strumming her ribs.

Scott looked on enviously. "Emily isn't ticklish."

The first time a boy tries to tickle me I stand still, pretending it has no effect on me, even though it does. They give up pretty easily. I figure there's a lot of little ways a girl can protect herself. Lindsay doesn't seem to get it. In third grade boys threw spitballs at her in class and chased her on the playground at recess. I used to be jealous of the attention and couldn't figure out why boys "liked" Lindsay and not me. It took me a few years to realize I didn't want that kind of attention and the boys had just figured it out before I had.

"Nooooooo!" Lindsay screamed, then laughed. Her body went slack and she slid off the chair. Her face turned bright pink when she found herself on the floor of the cafeteria.

Carlos helped her up, raising her by the armpits. He hugged her and she shoved him away. She took a step back and they looked at each other. Carlos's mischievous brown eyes are fringed with a flock of lashes it's just not fair for a guy to have. He can be very sweet, but he's also a pain. He made me appreciate Scott, who was so steady. I always knew what to expect of him. I wished I could change his views on Iraq, but I knew that probably wouldn't happen.

***

I had some free time during sixth period so I wrote a letter to our newly elected congressman, Cal Dooley. He was a farmer and the shining hope of local growers who wanted their views represented in Congress. I had no idea how Dooley felt about going to war in the Persian Gulf when I wrote this:

November 30, 1990

Dear Congressman Dooley:

I am writing you in regards to the crisis in the Persian Gulf. I don't want our country to go to war. Hundreds of thousands of young Americans could die over there. I don't want any Iraqis to die either. The detonation of so many weapons could damage our world's fragile ecology. Please vote against going to war.

Sincerely,
Emily Rankin

p.s. We are growers like yourself. Our crop is oranges.
p.p.s. I am too young to vote, but I won't be next election. My parents both voted for you and my dad never votes Democrat.

I read over the letter and thought it ended a bit too informally. It was the kind of tone I would use to write to a friend. Then I thought why can't I write to my congressman like a friend? He represents me to my government; he darn well better be my friend! I folded my letter purposefully, feeling like it could save the world.

After school I went to the Tulare County Library to do a couple of hours of research for Connell. We had planned to get together the next day so I could give her my week's worth of photocopied magazine articles and she could tell me which magazines she wanted me to look in next.

When I got home Connell called and said, "Don't bother driving into town tomorrow. You can give me your research at the peace vigil on Sunday."

It was hard for me to speak up to Connell, but I knew I had to. "I'm not sure I'm going. I mean, I can't get anyone to go with me. I probably won't know anyone there."

"You'll know me."

"I mean other kids."

"Ah, peers. Perhaps I'm being too presumptuous here. Just because you're my assistant doesn't mean you subscribe to my politics." A chill crept into her voice that caused my heart to speed. This was a sort of tactic of hers: her words were soothing but her tone was threatening to hold me at a distance.

"Oh, but I do agree with your politics! I mean, I believe we should try to avoid going to war. It's just that...oh, I don't know." But I did know and so did Connell: I lacked the courage to stand up for my convictions.

"Let's leave it open then," she said, her tone warming again. "If I don't see you at the peace vigil we can make other arrangements for our work together."

"Okay." I was about to add "goodbye," but Connell had already hung up.

***

At dinner that night I told my parents, "I want to go to this peace thing on Sunday, but I'm afraid I'll be the only kid there from my school."

"What peace thing?" asked Mom.

"You know how the UN has given Iraq that January 15 deadline to get out of Kuwait? Well, maybe if enough people protest, then the president won't start a war."

"War seems pretty inevitable, Em," said Dad. "That Hussein is a madman. He has to be stopped, all his nasty chemical weapons destroyed."

"He can be stopped, Dad. By the sanctions. They need more time to work. And US intervention could mean Vietnam all over again."

"Oh, no, Emmie, don't worry about that," said Dad. "It'll all be over in a couple of weeks."

"My own little girl! Protesting a war." Mom patted me on the back of the hand.

"Break out your old peace sign button and love beads, Mommy," said Dad.

"Since when have you become so socially conscious?" she asked.

"We've been studying the Persian Gulf in history class."

"Isn't it supposed to be the American Civil War? This is about that history teacher again, isn't it?"

"Well, Dr. McKenzie is the one who made me aware of the situation, but I've drawn my own conclusions."

Mom shook her head, muttering, "Such an impressionable age."

I set down my fork and leaned toward Mom. "How come you can't stand Dr. McKenzie? You ought to be glad I have such a good teacher. She knows more than any teacher I ever had."

"She's okay. I just wish she'd stick to the curriculum. I don't approve of her filling your head with ideas."

"What's wrong with ideas? Gee, Mom, I always thought you liked me to think about things."

Mom raised a shoulder, then dropped it, dismissing the subject. I felt torn. My mom didn't see how great my favorite teacher was, and it actually hurt my feelings. Maybe she was jealous. Mom and I had always been so close. I had never had an adult woman as a friend. I'd definitely never had a teacher for a friend. *Was* Connell my friend? It certainly felt like it.

"What sort of protest are you talking about, Emmie?" Daddy reached for a second biscuit.

"It's not a protest, it's a peace vigil." I explained how the group was planning to hold up signs on the corner of Mooney and Walnut.

The look on my dad's face made me afraid he was going to say I couldn't go. "I'd rather see you steer clear of any protest. This is a conservative community. A lot of people would resent any anti-war demonstrations. They would consider it un-American, an insult to the president. Some yahoos always looking for a fight could make trouble. You could get hurt."

"Ah, Daddy, you're just overprotective. You really believe someone would beat me up for holding a peace sign?"

He nodded. "Or threw a beer bottle at you or even take a pot-shot at you."

"I'm supposed to be afraid to stand up for my beliefs in my own little town? Cower before the almighty President of the United States?"

"We *did* elect him. It's better to stand by his decision, like it or not."

Mom looked at Daddy and stopped a laugh with the back of her hand.

"Don't you tell, Bunny. If you tell, I'll tell."

"Tell what, Dad?" asked Ryan, his mouth full of mashed potatoes. I didn't think he was even listening, but he's pretty smart for eight, and he could sense some good information coming up.

"It's nothing," Dad said.

"It is," I said. "Tell us yourself, Dad."

Mom's eyelashes fluttered at Dad. She had this goofy look on her face, which I like to see because it tells me she still loves him a whole lot.

"Okay." Dad crossed his knife and fork neatly across his plate, like he was about to make some major announcement. "I know this is hard for you to believe, Em, but I was once young, too. I didn't have as much sense as you, though."

I laughed. I couldn't imagine my dad being irresponsible about anything. "So what did you do?"

"Burned my draft card."

"What a rebel!" said Mom. "He did it after the war. After the draft had been called off." She slapped the table, tears forming she was laughing so hard.

"I oughta tell the kids what you burned."

Mom shook her head, still laughing. "No, don't."

"What'd you burn, Mommy?" Ryan asked.

"Her bra," said Dad.

"Really?" said Ryan. "Which one? How come?"

"It stunk and then Daddy bought me a new one."

"Damn right. I didn't want my girl ending up with a pair of string beans."

"Oh, Daddy, that's gross!" I slapped his arm.

"I don't get it," said Ryan.

"You don't want to," I said. "Serious, Daddy, how did you stay out of Vietnam?"

"Same way most well-off guys did. I had a student deferment most of the time, and then a fairly high lottery number."

"Did you think the US was right being involved in Vietnam?"

"Yep. It was about the free world against communism."

"Oh, please!" said Mom, wiping her eyes on her napkin. "If you were so gung ho, why didn't you enlist?"

"I didn't want to stumble around some stinking jungle and get shot at."

"That's not fair, Daddy. You wanted other guys to die there instead?"

"I never wanted to be a hero, Em, especially a war hero. Lots of guys like combat. They'll give you some high ideals about the reason they're fighting, but the truth is they like shooting guns and flying jets. Gives them something to talk about."

"Maybe some," said Mom. "But a lot of guys that died in Vietnam never wanted to be there in the first place. A lot of them were poor blacks from the South with no money for college. They never knew what hit them. Just doing their duty to God and country and—boom—they're dead. Some of the survivors are even worse off than the dead ones."

"That's Gary," I said.

"It's a damn shame," said Daddy. "He was a couple grades ahead of me, but I sorta knew him. Good athlete. I think he made every team Redwood High had."

"Is he in counseling?" Mom asked.

"In and out lots of times. It doesn't seem to help."

"Vietnam was a long time ago," said Dad. "What he needs is hard work—work he can believe in. Maybe a wife and kids."

"You're oversimplifying, Sam," Mom said. "You just don't know what demons the poor man carries around with him. I'm glad they're not running around inside your head. You're damn lucky you never got the grand tour of Southeast Asia."

We were all quiet for a while.

"Anyway, Mom, about the peace vigil, will you go with me?"

"Oh, no, I'm afraid not."

"Well, that's a relief," said Dad. "It's one thing having my teenaged daughter seen around town acting like a lunkhead. My wife is another."

"A lunkhead? Oh, Daddy, you sound like Grandpa. And I don't get you, Mom. You're all anti-war at college, then marry a conservative rancher, move to Visalia, and become pro-war?"

"It's not that simple—pro-war or anti-. You've got to examine each situation. I hope we don't have a war in the Persian Gulf, but maybe we'll just have to. You do what you have to, Emmie, but I agree with Daddy this time. Hussein has to be stopped. Besides, I don't think Dr. McKenzie's protest will do any good. It certainly won't change anyone's mind around here."

It's not Dr. McKenzie's protest, I wished I could tell her, but I didn't want to bring up her name again and watch my mother's face get all tense. I was disappointed Mom wouldn't go with me, but something about discussing the peace vigil with my parents helped me make up my mind about it.

The next hard part was making a sign. I found some old poster board in my closet and got out my markers. I didn't know what to write. On a sheet of binder paper I tried out "Stop George Bush. No war on January 15th." Too long. People could never read the whole thing just driving by. Then I tried "Not another Vietnam." I remember how Mom said you can't generalize all wars. Finally I just wrote "PEACE." Not very original, but it worked for me.

I didn't have the heart to nail the poster to a stick. It reminded me too much of Christ's crucifixion and then my own if any of my friends happened to drive by and see me standing there with all the peaceniks. I figured I'd just hold the sign in front of me like a shield—although a shield that would invite danger rather than ward it off. I placed the sign in the back of the car facedown—as if its message were an obscenity.

6

Connell pulled into the Grand Auto parking lot on Walnut Avenue at the same time I did, about 1:05. We parked side by side. I searched the area, half expecting a store employee to be patrolling the lot, telling protesters they couldn't park there.

I heard a rap on the driver's window and rolled it down. Connell was standing there holding a "No Blood for Oil" sign. "Looking for someone?"

"Oh, uh, no." I got out of the car and went around back to get my sign. I opened the hatchback, then froze, feeling exposed. Ashamed. People who knew me, my family, would see me. They would be shocked and smug. Tongues would wag at church, at the country club: "Wait until you hear this..." "That Emily Rankin, a troublemaker now, a radical. I saw her at that war protest and..." "A very spoiled girl. I knew Sam and Bunny gave her too much. Now look what she's become..."

"Coming, Emily?" Connell was already a few steps ahead of me.

"Uh, sure." I pulled out my poster and shut the hatchback. I held the sign facedown against my leg and hurried after Connell.

Cool air hit me on all sides. I was out in the open! No sniper's bullet whistled toward my heart, no bolt of lightning struck me dead. Now I was walking with my history teacher—so beautiful, so brilliant—my favorite person. Now I was smiling. I looked toward the row of about twenty ordinary-looking people, dressed in ordinary jeans and jackets, hats and mittens. I recognized only one person—the children's librarian at the county library who had always saved me the very best books as soon as they came in. Suddenly it was okay. I was okay. This must be what it feels like to go to a nude beach: at first you're ashamed, a little embarrassed, and then you look around and everyone else is as exposed as you, so what's the big deal?

The other protesters greeted us cheerfully. Many of them were elderly, something I found comforting. They had lived through many wars, including War World II. They knew from experience that war should be avoided.

One of the elderly women was in a wheelchair. She held a sign that said "Peace on Earth," the same words you'd read on a Christmas card. The difference was she meant it. I figured a lot of people would send that same message out as their holiday greeting, thinking, "I wish there could be peace, but because President Bush believes there should be a war, of course we can't have peace." Christians believe God is on their side, but so do Muslims. People are always using God as an excuse to kill each other. It must make Him sad. I believe He just wants us all to get along and be happy.

I found out many of the protesters were Quakers. They called themselves "Friends." It's against their religion to do violence to anyone, even in war. One mother was accompanied by her two young children, a preschool girl who held a well-worn pink stuffed bunny under her arm, and a blonde toddler boy strapped into a stroller, the youngest protester in sight. The mother held a sign reading "Earth: Love it or leave it." The adults seemed to range in age from seventy to twenty. The only age group missing was my own.

Connell and I selected a hunk of sidewalk and held up our signs. A woman with long black-and-gray hair and horn-rimmed glasses came down the row of protesters passing out yellow ribbons. Handing me a ribbon and safety pin she said, "We need to support the US troops, but not the war. We want them to come home safe. My boy is in the army, stationed in Saudi Arabia."

This surprised me. I thought all the parents of enlisted guys were always gung ho about war, that they had presented their boys with a new GI Joe every Christmas and birthday, telling them in hushed reverence, "Maybe some day you'll be a war hero, too."

But not this lady with the yellow ribbons. She explained, "I tried to warn Tom, but no, he wouldn't listen to his mother. He told me, 'Mom, I'm just going in for my college education.' My husband and me didn't have the money to send him ourselves. You know those army recruiters lurking outside of high school gyms promise those kids the world. They even run those commercials during Saturday morning cartoons, trying to brainwash toddlers. I told him, 'Tommy, it's just not worth it. If our country gets in a war, you'll be the first to go.' Sure enough, George Bush is about to send my boy into action."

The woman moved on, telling everyone about her son, offering her ribbons. It was the first I had heard about yellow ribbons symbolizing US troops in the Persian Gulf War. I wondered who started the idea, which must have been borrowed from that old song "Tie a Yellow Ribbon 'Round the Old Oak Tree," about a man coming home from prison, I think, who asks his girlfriend to tie a ribbon around a tree trunk if she still loves him and wants him back, and she ends up tying ribbons around a hundred trees.

I formed the yellow ribbon into a bow and pinned it to my jean jacket lapel, thinking it was a nice gesture. Perhaps the troops' presence in the Middle East would keep the peace, causing Hussein to withdraw from Kuwait without a fight. I really did wish for the soldiers' safe return.

Connell had accepted the ribbon, but when the woman moved on, she slipped it into her pocket. I thought she either didn't feel like taking off her gloves to tie it in a bow or, lost in a discussion with the person next to her, she may not have even noticed it was placed in her hand.

Visalia usually has little traffic, yet a steady stream of cars passed us that afternoon. Most of them were filled with Christmas shoppers, stuck at the light at Mooney and Walnut, waiting to cross the intersection and turn into the mall.

It was interesting to watch the people read our signs. Their foreheads tensed, their lips moved. Few of them seemed to have any idea why we were there. Some shook their heads in disagreement. Others looked away, embarrassed for themselves or for us. Some drivers honked their horns and flashed a two-finger V. When Nixon used to do that he meant "victory." I wonder how the gesture came to symbolize peace.

Once in a while someone driving by would shout, "Nuke Iraq!" It was always some guy in his late teens or early twenties in a car with a bunch of other young guys, drawing the courage to yell the same way they might go off to war—having strength in numbers. I didn't know any of them. In fact, I didn't recognize a single person all afternoon.

The hour passed quickly. By the end of it I had that same smug, righteous feeling I got picking up someone else's litter at a campground—helping out, however small. I had done my part in saving the world.

Connell was less optimistic. "I expected a poor turnout around here, but that was pathetic. I counted twenty-three people."

We were seated at her kitchen table, warming our hands on mugs of steaming tea.

"Maybe more people will show next Sunday," I said, "after the word gets around."

"After all my lecturing! Not a single one of your classmates!"

"Most of us come from fairly conservative backgrounds. Protesting a war seems pretty radical to most of them."

Connell reached across the table and placed her hand over mine. "It took a lot of courage, huh?"

"At first. I'm okay about it now. Proud, even."

"Well, I'm proud of you, too," she said. I had only a split second to bask in the glow of her approval before she added, "Now let's see you bring five more kids with you next week."

"I don't see how I can talk anyone into something they don't want to..." I trailed off, distracted by her fingering my lapel. At first I didn't realize what she was doing. Then the safety pin came unfastened and she held my little yellow bow in her palm.

"Don't wear this anymore. It means you're pro-war."

"But the woman said—"

"You're either for the war or against it, Emily. It's black or white, no gray areas here. I'm truly sorry for that woman, but I don't believe her son is as innocent as she does. A person who enlists in the military becomes a hired killer."

"Wow, isn't that pretty harsh? If we didn't have a good defense system other countries would attack us."

"Yes, but we don't need so much defense. We put billions and billions of dollars into the military and those generals get pretty bored keeping the peace. After a while they get to feeling a little ridiculous. They need a war to justify their existence. They get antsy to use up that stockpile of weapons the government eked out of our schools, our highways, the arts. Now Bush needs a reason to be reelected."

"I don't believe that! A president wouldn't start a war just to get reelected."

"A president has never been voted out of office during a war. The presidency is power. And once a man has that much power he'll do anything to hold on to it. I know what it's like, Emily, I've been there. I've stood on Capitol Hill, I've delivered papers to Congress. I've seen what power does to men."

"Wow, Connell, you've spoken to Congress?!"

"Ah, just a congressional subcommittee on the anti-war movement in '74. They get outside people to come in all the time. Both my husband and I spoke at that one."

My eyes fluttered over the fourth finger of her left hand, even though I already knew it was bare. She had never mentioned a husband before so I figured she must have meant an ex-husband.

1974 was a long time ago. I wanted to ask her about him but didn't have the nerve. Instead I asked, "Connell, what are you doing in Visalia?"

She laughed. "It's a job."

"You should be teaching at a university."

She shrugged. "I apply all the time, but there's a freeze on hiring most everywhere. A position at San Francisco State had five hundred applicants. Grant money and fellowships for the type of book I'm writing are scarce, too, though I keep trying. I'm lucky I don't have to wait tables to support my writing."

"There's high schools back East."

"Of course, but I wanted to come here, Tulare County, one of the poorest counties in the nation. I want to try to understand you people."

I stared into my tea, feeling insulted. Connell made herself sound like an anthropologist here to study the pygmies. I knew we were a poor county; there were the migrant farmworkers moving from one crop to another to make a meager living, plus the unemployed and uneducated. But they were a part of the population that didn't really touch my life, even though many of them worked on our ranch. I always thought of the San Joaquin Valley as the land of plenty, overflowing with citrus, milk, cotton, almonds, olives, tomatoes, and grapes. And I always thought of myself as a caring person. Now it looked like I was just another rich white girl oblivious to those less fortunate suffering around me.

I looked up at Connell. "You don't like us. You seem unhappy here."

"Not true! I'm glad I got a chance to teach at Orange Valley. Usually it's okay when I can get a class discussion going, but there seem to be so many kids who aren't interested in learning, who actually resent me for teaching them. One morning—you wouldn't believe it—I found my car smeared with all kinds of crap."

I tried to look innocent—I must have. I leaned forward and said, "You mean like real crap?"

She laughed. "No, some gooey orange matter. They'd written obscenities all over my car." She smiled and shrugged. "And a peace sign."

"Was it Silly String?"

"I don't know, maybe."

"I'm sorry, Connell. Did it wash off easily?"

"I don't know. I took it to the car wash—no harm done. I guess I wasn't being singled out. It's just what teachers put up with these days." She pushed a platter of chocolate chip cookies toward me. "It's all been worth it. I got to meet you, Emily. I'm glad I have you to talk to."

"Have you made friends with any of the other teachers?"

"Of course, but they're all so busy, most of them married with families, and I'm busy with my writing. You've been a great help to my work."

I shrugged. "Just photocopying magazine articles? That's easy."

"Easy for you because you're organized and a self-starter. I've had to hold hands with more than one research assistant and they were college students."

"Well, then thanks."

"You're quite amazing, a real enigma: 'A' student, research assistant, war protester, cheerleader."

"I've never tried to fit any particular stereotype."

"Oh, but my dear, cheerleading?! That perpetuates the male chauvinistic tradition that men 'do' while women serve."

I'd heard it all before—it was what I would expect from someone like Connell. "It's not just about girls cheering for boys. Cheerleading takes a lot of practice and skill. It's a sport, like any other."

"I suppose if you didn't have male football players and basketball players to cheer for you'd still be jumping up and down?"

"Well, yeah. Our squad competes in cheerleading meets all over the state. We hold the AACC title in the Southern California Division."

"Oh? Well, even so, the social implications are—"

"I don't care," I interrupted, feeling the heat rise under my shirt. "I love cheerleading. It's a good workout and it's fun. I like all the girls on our squad and I get to perform and keep up with some of my gymnastics."

"You're a gymnast, too?"

"Was. I quit when I reached the point where I'd have to practice three or four hours a day to get any better. Anyway, I have the wrong body type." I glanced down at my breasts. "I think some judges would deduct points just because I bounced around too much."

She lectured me some more about consciousness-raising, but I just let it flow over me like a hot wind. After a while she gave up and we got down to work. I handed over my thick stack of copies, and she paid me for the week's work and gave me a list of the periodicals she wanted me to look into the following week.

Driving home, I went over the day in my mind and a warm, liquid feeling of satisfaction coursed through my veins. I had stood up for peace for the first time; it took some courage, and I was growing closer to Connell. I wasn't a bit worried that she disapproved of cheerleading; we didn't have to see eye to eye on everything. I was, in fact, pleased with myself for standing my ground. A war-protesting cheerleader—that made me smile. Wasn't that a sign of strong character, deciding for myself what I should believe in?

The important thing was that Connell truly liked me. She thought of me as a friend, and she had almost said as much. Emily Rankin: a personal friend of someone who had spoken before the United States Congress.

***

I attended the peace vigils for the next several weeks but I never did recruit those other five students. I didn't even try. I'd never convince any of my group to join me. If I mentioned it to Scott, I figured we'd just fight about it. I didn't tell Lindsay or Skylar or any of my friends on the cheerleading squad, which seems kind of weird now that I think back, but it wasn't then. My participation in the peace vigils was like a separate part of me that didn't have anything to do with my social life at school.

Each week it got colder standing out in the open for an hour holding my peace sign. The chill in the cement sidewalk seemed to travel up my legs and settle in my hip bones. I had to stamp my feet just to feel them. I couldn't ever remember being that cold in Visalia.

And it got colder.

Each Sunday a few more people showed up. By the third week we swelled to a whopping fifty-four. Some other teens made an appearance, kids I didn't know, maybe from the other two high schools in town. A reporter from the *Visalia Times-Delta* interviewed some of us kids.

The headline in the local section of the following Monday's paper read "Local Teens Protest US Presence in Gulf," and appearing with it was a photo of us huddled together, smiling into the camera and flashing our splayed-finger peace signs. I was quoted as saying, "I don't want any young Americans to have to fight in a war and die. I want all the US troops to come home safe and whole." I was thinking of Gary when I'd said that.

Scott was leaning against my locker when I got to school. His hair was still wet from the shower he took after lifting weights with some of the other basketball players that morning. The part in his hair stood out, a narrow line of white skull. It made me think how vulnerable human heads are, how easily they can be cracked. He held the newspaper up to my face.

"What gets me the most is I had to read about it instead of you just telling me."

"I'm sorry, Scott. I figured you didn't want to talk about it, and you know how I feel about this war."

"Yeah, but I never believed you'd go and do this!" His grip tightened, crumpling the photo. My legs disappeared into his fist, my face rippled. "Do you have any idea what the guys put me through this morning? And what about my uncle Gary? Don't you have any respect for him? You think he wasted his life for nothing?"

"I wish the Vietnam War never happened."

"Of course it had to happen, Emily. Don't be so damn naïve! You've been standing out there week after week and never said one damn word to me! My God, it's like I don't even know you anymore."

"Then maybe you never did."

"Fine. Let's just leave it at that!" He stalked off, the squeak of his rubber soles reverberating down the hall.

I blinked once, twice, my eyes stinging, my cheeks burning.

***

Third period I got to Connell's class early, thinking I could talk to Scott there, the only class we had together. He walked in after the bell. He took his seat next to me without looking my way. I tore a sheet out of my notebook and wrote "Leave what at what?" I folded it twice and set it on his desk. Connell began to lecture, watching Scott slowly unfold the note. He read it, folded it back up, and slid it into his pocket, staring straight ahead. I stopped watching him then. I wrote down whatever Connell scrawled on the board, forming letters into words that had no meaning to me. At last the bell rang, and I gathered up my books, determined to follow Scott out of class and make him talk this out.

"Emily," Connell called to me, "may I see you a moment?"

I looked up at her, then at Scott, who was shaking his head.

"Great article," she said. "You must be proud."

"I don't know. I feel exposed. A kid in my anatomy class called me a traitor. I don't even know him." I looked toward the door. Scott was gone.

"Well, it's not always easy to stand up for your convictions."

"Yeah. I'm finding that out."

She pressed my shoulder. "I'm proud of you, if that helps."

It didn't, not really.

At lunch I took one step into the cafeteria and stopped. Across the room I spotted Scott and Lindsay seated at our group's usual table, her elbow resting on his shoulder as she offered him a chip. This was nothing unusual; they looked like they did every other day at lunch, waiting for Skylar, Carlos, me, and the rest of our group to join them. Still, something in the way they looked into each other's faces made my legs too weak to cross the length of floor between them and me.

I turned and walked back down the hall, not knowing where I was headed. I thought if I ran into Skylar or Roger or Carlos—anyone in our group—and walked with them up to Lindsay and Scott I'd be okay, but I didn't see any of my friends so I bought a pack of M&M's out of a machine and dumped them loose in my coat pocket. I spent the period in the library, beneath the "No Eating or Drinking" sign, sneaking the M&M's one at a time, crunching the hard coating and letting the bits of chocolate dissolve on my tongue. I wasn't close to tears, just hurt and confused. I read a trashy *People* magazine one word at a time without linking them together to make sense, thinking we're not over yet, we can't end like this. There'd be tears and words, angry, thoughtful, or sad words, not this creepy silence.

In fifth period chemistry a rumor was going around that Scott had invited Lindsay to Winter Formal. So much for childhood friendships.

***

After school I was walking toward the office to call my mom to pick me up when I felt a strong arm go around my shoulders and squeeze me close. I rolled my eyes over to Carlos. "What are you doing?"

"Driving you home. My guess is you can use the ride."

I whirled around to get out of his embrace, even though a friendly hug felt pretty nice about then. "It's twenty miles round-trip. That's a lot of gas."

"Good point. You can buy me a burger and we'll call it even."

It was a relief to finally be talking about this, even though it was with Carlos instead of Scott. At the fast-food place I ordered him a whole meal and a diet soda for myself.

"Thanks, babe." Carlos took an obscenely large bite of burger and chewed enthusiastically. "I'm starved. Spent all of lunch looking for you. Wanted to ask you to Winter Formal." His mouth was so full I wasn't sure I'd heard right. He swallowed and peered up at me through his thick lashes, a dribble of sauce running down the side of his mouth. "Well?"

I handed him a napkin. "No, thanks."

"Come on, Emily. You know our whole group is going together. You don't want to miss the fun. I'll ask Lindsay to slow dance, Scott will ask you—bingo—everything is back the way it's supposed to be. You'll get what you want, I'll get what I want, or at least some of it."

"So. You just want to use Lindsay?'

"What a distasteful expression. She gets what she wants, too."

I shook my head. "I'm too hurt. I know Scott was mad at me, but to ask Lindsay to the dance when he's with me and to have her accept... These are friends? This is how friends treat each other?"

"Ah, now, Emily, Big Scott was just trying to show you who the man is."

"That's pretty sexist."

"And he's such a pussycat. Already he regrets it. The main man is just a poor victim of his own biology. Women, see, use both sides of their brains at the same time, while men can't. Women can feel, speak, and think all at the same time. Guys act, then think."

I rolled my eyes. "Oh, please. Since when did you study the brain?"

"I know stuff." True, Carlos has plenty of smarts, he just doesn't use them much. He has four brothers way older than him, all in med school or majoring in math or something hard, and then there's Carlos, the baby. I remember his mom wailing to my mom in the produce section of Vons, "A doctor's son and he gets nothing but Cs and Ds."

Carlos jammed a handful of fries into his mouth and talked and chewed at the same time. "Listen, it's true. Look at the car insurance companies. Why do you think boys have to pay twice as much as girls? It's based on scientific fact: guys are naturally reckless drivers. They are impulsive and do stupid things, then regret it later. You should have heard the ribbing Scott got in the weight room this morning. He was so pissed off he had to lash out at you. If he hadn't seen you until lunch this might never have happened. You and Big Scott belong together. He loves you, babe."

"He told you that?"

"Course not." He took another big bite of his burger and chewed thoughtfully. "Do you think guys say stuff like that to other guys? I can just tell, anyone can. Come on. We'll go to the dance as friends."

"I don't know who my friends are anymore."

He leaned forward, tapping his chest. "I'm not being your friend here?"

"You're being nice, Carlos, nicer than I ever thought you could be. But no thanks."

"Great! Now I don't have a date either."

"Take Skylar."

"Already been asked. She's going with some dweeb from band. All the hot girls I know have been asked."

"What took you so long? If you wanted to go with Lindsay why didn't you ask her weeks ago?"

"I wanted her to sweat it out a little. Make her really want me."

"You're too much."

"What's Scott's excuse?"

"We've been together eight months! I just assumed he was taking me."

"You know all about 'assume.'"

"Please, don't say it." I clapped my hands over my ears and still I heard it.

"'Assume' is making an 'ass' out of 'u' and 'me.'"

***

That night Lindsay called and started right in without a hello.

"Don't hate me, I can explain everything. It's just that Scott was all mad at you and I was all mad at Carlos so I'm all let's show them both and go to Winter Formal together, so don't be pissed at Scott 'cause, really, I'm the one that asked him."

Well, that made me feel a little better, so I shifted the receiver to the other ear and asked, "Who's calling, please?"

"Don't be like that. I called Carlos to tell him to ask you to Formal, but he said he already asked and you won't go. I can't believe you're being so selfish. You're going to wreck everything."

Me selfish? Well, that was typical Lindsay logic for you. She'd left a few things out of her narrative, like how much it hurt me and how self-serving this whole plan of hers was.

After a long pause she said, "Well, aren't you going to say anything?"

"Who is this?"

"Oh, you bitch!"

"I'm sorry, there's no one here by that name." I felt some vindication in the decisive click the receiver made when I set it in its cradle.

7

On Thursday when I walked in the back door after school, I found my mom at the sink, fixing dinner. I said hi to her, but she didn't answer me. She held the peeler suspended over a potato, staring trancelike out the window. Her stillness alarmed me. I walked over to see what she was looking at.

"What's Daddy doing out there picking all by himself?" I asked. He never picked anymore. I knew the first crew was scheduled to come in next Wednesday, the day after Christmas.

Mom dropped her jaw and paused. "He says it's going to freeze."

"So we'll run the wind machines all night like last night."

Mom turned to me. She was pale and her eyes were wide. I had never noticed so many wrinkles around her eyes. "Your dad says they won't do any good this time. It doesn't warm up during the day and the cold air goes up too high. There's no inversion layer."

The propellers on our thousand wind machines, which churned warm air down into the trees, were forty feet high. I didn't know a cold front could go higher than that. "But he put water in the furrows."

Mom shook her head. "That didn't work either. We've just had too many years of drought. The ground is too dry for it to do any good."

It was slowly sinking in: total devastation. One hundred percent of our crop was still on the trees—the navels, which were harvested in winter, and the still-green valencias, our summer crop.

"Where's Manuel? Why hasn't he gotten a crew together?"

"He and Daddy argued this morning."

I couldn't believe it. Manuel Morales had been our ranch manager longer than I could remember. Grandpa had hired him years before he'd passed the ranch onto Daddy. Manuel always gave his opinion and my dad always listened to it, but in the end Dad was the boss and Manuel followed his directions.

"Manuel told Daddy it was no use, the sugar content isn't high enough yet. The oranges would be red-tagged anyway. But Daddy tested the fruit this morning. He said it should pass inspection."

"Then what are we standing here for?"

"I have to get dinner."

I had once seen my mom throw a pot of boiling spaghetti in the sink where it stuck like a gelatinous glop because Dad had shouted "Wind machines!" All four of us had dashed out to the groves to rev them up. Even Ryan knew how to pull the throttle and push the start button that was positioned on the post of each machine. Now Mom acted paralyzed.

"I'll call Scott. Maybe he can round up some of the other guys." It didn't worry me that he and I hadn't spoken in four days. I knew he would help us if he could.

Mom followed me to the phone. "Wait. Those kids will pull the buttons off. We'll have to dump the fruit anyway."

"I can teach them how to pick in two minutes flat."

Mom pressed the plunger on the phone. "Better not interfere. Your dad may not like it."

I knew what she meant. Dad didn't like to ask favors. He was reluctant to let people in on his troubles. Even when he went into Sanger most mornings at five to have breakfast at the cafe with the other ranchers, he listened to what he called "the scuttlebutt" but contributed little more than a comment on the weather. But this time everyone would know his troubles. Every grower in the valley would have the same problem.

I punched out Scott's number, thinking that the worst thing that could happen is that Dad would blow his top and order the guys off his property, but it didn't seem likely.

"Scott, it's me."

"Emily. What?" His voice sounded hopeful but guarded.

"Mom says the oranges aren't going to survive the night. We need you right now. Can you come?"

"Of course."

"What about some of the other guys? Can you make some phone calls?"

"Sure, but I don't know who can come on such short notice."

"Do what you can and get over here."

I was about to hang up when Scott said, "Oh, Emmie, will your dad pay? Not me, I don't care, but some of the other guys will want to know."

I actually wasn't sure. Dad wasn't hiring them. He never hired teenagers, only Hispanic farm laborers who had families to support, who were capable of working three times as hard as most Anglo kids. I thought of the money Connell had paid me and figured I could use that. "Sure, we'll pay."

After I put down the receiver I went into my room and put on my ski clothes—thermal underwear and socks on the inside and nylon shell pants, parka, earmuffs, hat, and scarf on the outside. In the packing shed I pulled on work gloves and slung a canvas picking bag over my shoulder. I walked out to the groves, stood next to my dad, and reached for an orange.

"What are you doing out here, Emily? Get back in the house. It's too cold."

"You're out here."

We didn't say anything more. The bitter wind whipped at the brittle leaves, which rattled like snakes. The ladder scraped against the frozen ground when Daddy moved it. The oranges made dull thuds as they came to rest in my picking bag. For each one, I thought, I saved you, I saved you.

About a half hour later the Mustang's headlights flashed across the trees. It was only around five but already dark.

"Better wash up now," said Dad. "Your beau's here."

I kept picking. Scott walked up to us. He avoided my eyes but observed the way my picking bag was draped diagonally across my body, coming to rest on my hip. He took a bag off the forklift and put it on. Dad hesitated a moment, watching him, then continued to work.

"No one else was around," Scott said in a low voice. "Sorry, Em."

"Thanks for trying. Thanks for coming." I showed him how to grab the orange and twist so that the stem broke off above the button. He worked slowly at first, too carefully, and then increased his speed. Later I caught my dad watching him as he extended his long, lanky arm to pluck oranges most people would need a ladder to reach.

Mom and Ryan joined us. Ryan made a game out of trading us empty bags for full ones. He dragged the full bags to the waiting bins and dumped in the oranges. It saved us some time and Ryan seemed to enjoy himself. He darted wildly from person to person when two of us needed his assistance at once. He made me feel weary. To be eight again! To have all that energy and no worries.

By five it was pitch black. Dad rigged up a floodlight on a portable generator and we kept picking. Around seven Ryan complained he was hungry.

"Want some dinner?" Mom asked Dad.

"Later."

Mom looked at Scott and me.

"We'll eat when Dad does," I said.

Mom went inside with Ryan. She came back out for an hour or so, then went back in to put Ryan to bed.

It got colder. Every once in a while I ran up and down the rows just to feel my feet. I wanted to quit, but I forced myself to stay with it as long as Dad did. I didn't dare ask when he planned on quitting; I knew he'd order me into the house. I wondered if he planned to go all night.

About eleven, Daddy said, "All right now. Let's knock off."

We finished filling the bags we were on and dumped the oranges into the bins. Dad reached for his wallet in his back pocket. "I want to pay you, Scott."

"No, sir. I did this to help your family."

Dad reached out and shook Scott's hand. And then, what really surprised me, his other arm came around Scott in a hug. Dad's forehead came to rest a moment on Scott's shoulder. I realized, of course, how much taller Scott was than Dad, but I never really paid attention to it until then, my dear Daddy looking old and broken. In a blur I saw Dad mount the forklift and drive the bins into the shed.

Scott looked around. Even in the misty darkness the fruit shone like orbs of dim light. "Are you really going to lose everything that's still on the trees?"

"Daddy thinks so."

He sighed, his breath like a milky cloud before him. "God."

"We've done what we can, I guess. Come in and eat. Get warm by the fire."

"Naw, I don't want to get comfortable. I should get home."

We walked to his car, side by side, not touching. I wondered where we stood with each other, but I guess we were too cold and tired to figure things out. I tried to grasp what I felt about him, and the word "gratitude" leaped into my mind and heart. I'd never forget Scott standing out with my family in the freezing cold, the darkest evening of our ranching lives.

His hands were thrust deep in his pockets and his head was bent down. He sniffled. Our noses and eyes were running from the cold. At his car I saw that he was crying. He picked me up in a fierce embrace, my back pressed against his car. His hands went up beneath my stocking cap, his fingers catching in my hair, and he pulled as if he were trying to get at me through my skull. We kissed, and our lips and faces were so numb we felt only pressure, solid flesh against flesh, our tears and snot mixing together.

He moaned. "Emily, Emily," and this, the freeze, and the war was too much to feel.

"Stop!" I cried out.

He gasped, squeezed me tighter, then backed off. I touched my knuckle to my nose, dabbing. He wiped his nose on the cuff of his jacket like a little kid. When people cry in movies they never have snot—how do they manage?

"Oh, Scottie!" I said, gently accusing.

"Look, I'll tell Lindsay it was all a mistake. She'll understand."

"It's not that easy. She's already bought her dress."

His face scrunched up. "So?"

"A girl who has bought her dress does not understand."

"So she can take it back! She can wear it some other time. It's just a dumb dress, for God's sake."

"No, it's not. See, when a girl is out shopping and she puts on the right dress—the one just for her in all the mall—she looks in the dressing room mirror and she sees it all—her hair done up and her man beside her in his tux and all her girlfriends circled around clasping their hands and telling you how beautiful you look and the reflection of those tiny little mirrors swirling on the walls and the smell of gardenias on your wrist corsage and the guy's after-shave, and that pressure, that heavenly pressure of a slow dance, and—"

"Jeez, me and Lindsay are just going as friends. We just wanted to make you and Carlos mad."

"Congratulations, you succeeded."

"Aw, Emily, why don't you go with Carlos?"

"No! Anyway, he's asked Naomi."

"Naomi?"

"The Italian exchange student."

"*That* Naomi? With the—" He drew all sorts of curves in the air.

I nodded grimly. Leave it to Carlos to get the hottest girl in school. "Go have your fun. I'll be home reading *Andersonville.*" I crossed my arms and stamped my feet.

He cupped my elbows, drawing me near. "I screwed up. I'm sorry. Are we still together?"

"When you get done dating other girls, I suppose we are."

He gathered me up and kissed me again. "I won't have a good time, I promise."

"You better not," I said.

8

The next day Dad managed to scrape together a picking crew of twenty, including himself, Manuel Morales, a few migrant workers, and some of our packers. On Saturday I joined the crew. It was the day I was supposed to get my nails and hair done for Winter Formal, so I was grateful for the hard physical labor to help me forget my own troubles and to make me too tired to care that I wasn't going to the dance with my friends.

It stayed below freezing all through the weekend, sometimes dipping into the teens. Sunday morning my family got up early and went out to inspect the damage.

Dad picked up an orange and plopped it into my hand. "Here, feel."

I squeezed with all my might but the fruit didn't give.

Dad sawed it open with his pocketknife. It was frozen through. He tossed the orange over his shoulder. "That's it, then."

Dad had been able to salvage about ten percent of the navels, most of which would only be good enough for juice. The rest of the oranges were gone. Ten months of work, nearly a year of picking and packing would never happen—it had all been wiped out in three days of very cold weather. The Big Freeze of '90. The freeze of the century.

It sunk in like a slow numbing. I looked at my parents but they didn't look at me. They didn't look at each other. Dad stared down at a frozen orange he was trying to crush with his boot, an orange that refused to be anything but round. Mom gazed across the acres and acres of unpicked oranges, frozen and dead. In time they would rot. Still they would hang on the trees, oddly out of place, like ornaments on a Christmas tree left up after January.

"Hey, this feels like a hardball!" shouted Ryan. He wound up, knee to chin, and threw a fastball. The orange ricocheted off a wind machine pole and soared through the kitchen window. Ryan's face went slack with horror. "Oops. I didn't mean it, Daddy. It was an accident."

My parents' eyes followed the tinkling of glass, but their expressions didn't change and neither one said anything to Ryan.

"Sorry, Mom. I'm in trouble, aren't I? Aren't I in trouble?"

Mom sighed. "It's just one more thing, Ryan. Try to be more careful."

We went inside to get ready for church. After I dressed, I came downstairs and waited in the family room for everyone else. I turned on the Christmas tree lights to see if it would cheer me up. It didn't. I thought about Lindsay slow-dancing in Scott's arms. From upstairs came sounds of a scuffle, running water, Ryan howling, and Mom yelling about his never scrubbing the back of his neck. The wind whistling through the jagged hole in the kitchen sink window probably caused Mom to give it to him extra hard. Dad was in the kitchen, trying to patch the broken pane with a piece of cardboard and duct tape.

When he finished he came to sit with me, still in his work clothes, a mug of coffee in his hand. He smiled wearily at me, my poor old Daddy, wrinkled, weathered, and rough, always willing to make the best of it, even when the best of it was the worse I had ever seen. Right then I felt so much love for him tears flooded my eyes.

"Oh, now, Emmie-Em, we're not that bad off. A man knows there's gonna be some bad years in the ranching business."

I dabbed my eyes with my knuckle, trying not to smear my mascara. "What a waste."

"Yep. It's the waste that will damn near kill me, having to sit and watch the whole crop rot. I'm worried about the laborers, too. No work for the next ten months. Most of them have kids in Mexico dependent on the paychecks they send home. They're going to feel this freeze in their tummies."

"What will they do?"

Dad shrugged. "State aid, federal aid for those that are US citizens. There's talk of getting the president to call this a national disaster. Mainly it's the community and the charities that are going to have to pitch in. You'll be seeing lots of food drives and clothing drives. Hell, we're not going to let our workers starve. It'll be rough, though. Those Mexicans are used to working."

"Hispanics, Daddy."

"They aren't used to sitting around. There will be trouble, no doubt. Drinking and fighting and car crashes."

Mom came down dressed for church. She looked over Daddy in his work clothes. "Sam, what good can you do now?"

"Crop's gone, sure. Now I got to work on saving the trees."

"The trees can die, too?" I asked.

Dad nodded. "Yep. Those thousand saplings we planted last spring are probably gone."

"Oh, Sam, no!" Mom slumped onto the sofa next to him. Her chin came to rest on her knuckles as she glared at the Christmas tree, loaded with loot. "My Lord, look at all this stuff."

We were supposed to have had a bumper crop, an extra big Christmas. I had hinted around for a computer of my own and some huge, heavy packages with my name on them made me think my wish might come true. Mom had secretly told me that she had finally given into Ryan over Nintendo—she would simply restrict the amount of time he spent at it. Leaning against the wall, four narrow oblong packages held new skiing equipment for us all. We had picked them out together one evening, but Mom still wrapped them and put them next to the tree.

She asked, "Do you think we can take some of it back?"

"No need to. About everything's been taken from us, Bunny. No point in taking away Christmas too."

"We do need something to cheer us up," said Mom. "We ought to throw a party or something."

"Somehow, I'm not in the party mood," said Dad.

Mom snapped her fingers. "I got it! We can throw a red-tag party. Invite all the ranchers."

"Now what in the hell is a red-tag party?" asked Dad.

"I'm not quite sure. I'm making it up as I go along." Mom's eyes were wide and lively, but there were purplish bags underneath them; it made her look sort of crazed. "I'll get some red tags from the Ag Department and send them out as invitations." She was talking about the notices placed on fruit that didn't meet market standards and had to be dumped.

"Now, Bunny, that's not funny," said Dad.

"Come on, Sam, where's your sense of humor? We can wear old, ragged clothes and serve beans!"

"It's a bad idea," said Dad. "Give it up."

"On New Year's Eve! Yes! That'll be perfect. We can all commiserate!"

"Don't do this, Bonita."

Mom kissed Dad's turned-down mouth. "Oh, Sam, it'll be fun, wait and see. Come on, kids, we'll be late for church."

Dad looked at me. "Help me out of this one, Emmie. Try and talk some sense into her."

I hated to hurt Mom's feelings, but I had to be honest. "Dad's right, Mom."

"What are we supposed to do? Act like sitting ducks?"

"We *are* sitting ducks," said Dad.

"All the more reason why we can't act like them." Mom tilted her chin and trotted to the door like she knew exactly what she was doing.

***

That afternoon at the peace vigil Connell said, "I didn't expect you."

I shrugged, trying to be brave. "Life goes on."

"How bad is it?"

"We lost everything," I said, my voice hard. It was a pretty vague statement. I wanted it to be that way. I wanted Connell to fear the worst for my family. I didn't believe it was in her to mourn rotten fruit, but I wanted her to feel some of our pain. She gave me a hug. It made me cry. I pushed away from her and walked down the sidewalk, giving her no time to pin me down on the details or attempt to make me see that the freeze was anything less than disastrous.

I saw Elena Ginsberg from Connell's class. "Hi," I said. "Good to see you here."

Elena's eyes popped behind her little round glasses. "I was out last week, too."

"You were?" I thought I noticed everyone, especially the teenagers. How had Elena seen me and I not seen her? "Dr. McKenzie will appreciate it. I think it makes her feel discouraged that she doesn't get through to more of her students."

"I believe in this. But it was hard to make time for it this weekend with all the homework with both our AP history and anatomy finals."

I nodded, having just realized she and I were in the same anatomy class.

"And I stayed out pretty late last night, too."

"Oh, yeah. Winter Formal. How was it?"

"Okay, I guess. I went with this one guy I didn't really like. The guy I really wanted to go with didn't ask me."

I had to laugh. "Join the club. Who got Winter King and Snow Queen?"

"Scott and Lindsay."

I looked down at the sidewalk. "Oh."

I felt her hand on my arm. "I'm sorry, Emily. I guess you didn't really want to hear that. I guess you and Scott aren't together anymore, huh?"

I barely knew Elena, but she seemed to know all about Scott and me. "I think we're okay, actually. We just had this stupid fight last Monday and it seemed like we weren't together so Scott decided to go to the dance with Lindsay. We're all friends, you know."

"It seemed that way. I mean, just friends. Scott didn't seem all that interested in her. He mostly sat around talking with a bunch of guys."

"Oh? How did Lindsay take it?"

Elena laughed. "She didn't seem to mind at all. She left pretty early with Carlos."

"What happened to Carlos's date, Naomi?"

"She left earlier than both of them...right after she whacked Carlos over the head with her purse."

We laughed together. "Thanks for the full report."

After the vigil Elena invited me to her house, and I ended up staying for dinner. She's Jewish, I found out, and her family was in the middle of celebrating Hanukkah, lighting the sixth candle on the menorah that night. I thought I would be intruding, but they made me feel welcome. Mrs. Ginsberg made latkes, a kind of potato pancake I'd never tasted before. They were crispy and delicious.

The Ginsbergs are a liberal family, something you don't see much in Tulare County. Both parents are lawyers and Elena's brother Isaac—same curly black hair and round glasses—was home on winter break from Harvey Mudd College. Elena's dad was really funny, cracking jokes about what he called "Bushisms," referring to the president. He and Elena had a competition over who could balance a teaspoon on their nose the longest, and I laughed until my side ached. It was fun to be part of someone else's family for an hour and forget the sadness surrounding my own home.

When I was about to leave, Mrs. Ginsberg hugged me like a daughter. "Shalom," she said. Peace.

9

Monday morning, Christmas Eve, Mom asked me to help her in the office processing layoff notices for our forty packers. I think she needed my moral support more than my checking off names and licking envelopes. It was a sad thing to do on Christmas Eve, but the sooner the workers had notices the sooner they could apply for unemployment.

Around eleven, Ryan burst into the packinghouse. He had spent the night at a friend's and was just getting home. He was wild-eyed and red-faced, looking like some man-eating monster had chased him through the groves. He put his hands on his knees, gasping so fiercely he could hardly get his words out. "It's...ra-raining."

Mom and I peered out the window. I expected Ryan to come back with "Ha ha, you fell for it," but he was still trying to catch his breath.

Mom said, "Very funny, silly-willy. Did you and Josh stay up all night? Why did you run all the way over here in the freezing cold?"

"In the house, Mom. It's just pouring."

"What do you mean?" she said. "Which part?"

"The family room. Water's coming down the wall like a big ol' waterfall."

Mom sprang from her chair. "Oh my God, the pipes! I thought Daddy wrapped them all."

On the drive home Ryan asked, "What makes it do that?"

"The water froze inside the pipes," I explained. "Water expands when it freezes, takes up more room. There wasn't enough room in the pipes for it, so the ice just broke them apart sometime last night without our knowing. When it gets warmer the running water gushes out of the pipes behind the wall."

Mom groaned at the image. "Oh, God. Not this."

"If Daddy wraps them, it's like a band-aid?"

"No, Ryan. It keeps the pipes warm enough so they don't freeze."

Mom pulled into the drive and we jumped out of the car. I beat Mom to the porch, unlocked the front door, and stepped in. I could feel her peering over my shoulder into the family room.

The room is a step down from the living room, and the step contained the water, making the family room into a giant wading pool, four inches deep. Some of our smaller Christmas presents bobbed on the surface like rubber ducks.

"Cool!" said Ryan.

Mom turned and dashed out of the house and around to the back to turn off the water main. "Go find Daddy," she yelled back at me.

It was hard to pull my eyes away from such a bizarre sight. "What next?" I asked no one in particular. Then I went out to the groves to look for Daddy.

***

In church on Christmas Day, I wished that Christmas could just stay put there and not follow us out into the world and back home. I just wanted to kneel before the Nativity scene, feel the holy joy of Jesus' birth, sing "Silent Night," and pray for peace. I wished no one had ever started the idea of Santa Claus and Christmas trees and exchanging gifts. I was too sad for all of that.

It took too much effort to act happy. Filing out of church, I wondered how we were going to get through the rest of the day.

At home around the breakfast table, Dad opened up the *Visalia Times-Delta,* read the inch-tall headline—"Ag Chief Forecasts $700 Million Loss"—and then folded the paper back up again and replaced the rubber band around it, as if bad news could simply go away if you didn't read it. But he wasn't quick enough. The $700 million loss jumped out at us all.

Mom stared at the folded newspaper. "I know what," she said slowly. "I'll make clown-face pancakes."

"Aw, Bunny, give us a break!" Dad placed his head in his hands, as if he couldn't bear the sight of two egg eyes, a butter-pat nose, and a bacon-strip smiley mouth staring back at him from his plate.

"It's been a long time since clown pancakes have worked on us, Mom," I said.

Ryan went up to her and put his arms around her waist. "I still like clown pancakes, Mommy."

She made up two plates of clown pancakes, two plain.

Dad had used the Shop Vac to suck up the water in the family room and then placed space heaters around to dry the carpet. Still, it smelled like a swamp and would have to be replaced. We didn't dare plug in the Christmas tree lights for fear of being electrocuted. Fortunately we didn't have to open presents. Mom had unwrapped them all the previous day to dry them out. My new computer and Ryan's Nintendo were water-damaged beyond repair. Mom said she would replace them if our homeowner's insurance covered their loss. My favorite gift was from her, one of the floaters that water couldn't hurt. She had dug through an old jewelry box and come up with her silver peace earrings from the sixties. She'd polished them up, although black tarnish was still caked in the inner curves because she was afraid they'd break if she rubbed too hard.

Later on, my Grandpa Harry and Grandma Lee drove down from Three Rivers to have Christmas dinner with us. They had retired up there after Grandpa passed the ranch onto Dad in a living trust deal about five years ago. Retire—that was a laugh! Grandpa could only take it about six months before he bought a flock of emus and started ranching them, and now at the age of seventy-six he was going to school for his realtor's license. Whenever he comes to visit he always tells Daddy everything he's doing wrong. This year Mom asked Dad if he wanted her to make an excuse to not have them for Christmas dinner, but Dad said it wasn't any use: Grandpa would want to see for himself the freeze damage and would have been down sooner if it hadn't been for Christmas coming up anyway. Grandpa and Dad toured the groves together, and when they came back into the house, Dad wasn't scowling or snapping one- or two-word answers at anybody, so I guess Grandpa went easy on him.

Scott stopped by around four so we could exchange gifts. I got him an official Kings cap and he got me a pin shaped like a waving flag, studded with red, white, and blue rhinestones.

My grandma said, "Oh, what a lovely brooch!" and I felt like saying You want it? Take it. It looks like something an old lady would wear.

I said, "Gee, thanks," and he sort of laughed, embarrassed.

"I just don't want you to forget how much you love your country."

Why would I? I don't know how the American flag came to mean war supporter. I used to think it was beautiful and I liked waving it around like everyone else.

Scott's mom makes him wear a suit and tie to church, and he was still dressed up like that, in his "Sunday best," straining his neck against the tight collar. We were both pretty stiff and uncomfortable sitting side by side in the living room with my grandparents and family. He didn't stay long. I couldn't tell if things were back to normal with us or not.

The only good thing about Christmas Day was that Grandma had gotten Ryan a remote control car, which he loved—his only present that wasn't soaked. Mom's roast beef was a little dry. I had two glasses of wine at dinner without anyone saying a word. I did all the dishes, then went to bed early with gruesome *Andersonville*.

Christmas 1990 was over—thank God.

***

Mom's Red-Tag New Year's Bash was even worse than I expected. Mom let me invite my group, but of course everyone but Scott went to Lindsay's family's annual New Year's Eve party. The Petersens invite half their church congregation and anyone their kids want, so it's huge, with all ages roasting wieners, playing charades and board games, and swing dancing fifties style. I've been attending it for years, but somehow this year I was happy I had my mom's red-tag party as an excuse not to go, even though her party was just for adults and, as I'd guessed, no fun at all.

My parents' guests showed up at our house in ragged clothes with red tags tied on their wrists. After they all yukked it up over each others' hobo outfits, there wasn't much to do. My mom buzzed around with a kind of hostess's fake party grin, sloshing jug wine into Mason jars and passing around tin plates of baked beans and corn bread.

People ate and ran. By ten o'clock the house was cleared except for my family and Scott.

Mom flopped backward onto the sofa, kicking her feet and wailing, "Grim! Horrible! The worst party in the history of the world." She covered her face with a throw pillow. "The pain! The agony! The humiliation!" She propped herself up on her elbow, the pillow sliding off her face. "Why didn't you guys try to stop me?"

Dad and I just looked at each other.

"Well, why didn't you try harder?"

Scott and I helped clean up, then cuddled on the sofa to watch New Year's Eve at Times Square. At midnight we kissed and said "Happy New Year."

"1991 is bound to be better than this," said Scott.

"I kind of doubt it." I couldn't imagine what it would be like—our ranch out of commission for nearly a year. Then there was impending war. It seemed like the worst year of my life was coming up.

I was right and I was wrong. How does the opening of *A Tale of Two Cities* go? "It was the best of times, it was the worst of times." Yeah, I would say it was like that.

10

Christmas break was so depressing I wished I was in school. Our family ski trip was canceled due to blizzard warnings in the Sierra. Not that anyone was in the mood to ski, but at least it would have been better than moping around the house. Dad lay on the sofa, hour after hour, not reading, not watching TV, just staring up at the ceiling. It was creepy. Sometimes I'd come down the hall thinking about other stuff and I'd be startled to see him there, eyes wide open, still as a corpse. Once I actually stood there a while, waiting for him to at least say hi, but it was like he didn't even see me.

Mom still went to the office every day, even though there wasn't much to do. I worried about her being over there all by herself so I made excuses to drop by. The immobile machinery seemed as if it hadn't operated in years. The quiet unnerved me, like the place was haunted. I wished I had made tape recordings of the sounds of production so I could play them in the office now. Mom joked, "The racket used to give me a headache. Now I have nothing to complain about."

She spent her evenings curled up by the fire with her *New Yorker,* cabernet sauvignon, and Hershey's Kisses. Often her eyes slipped off the page to stare into the flames. When it was Ryan's bedtime, she quietly told him to go get ready, and if he was slow doing it or skipped brushing his teeth, she didn't do anything about it. She said she was okay whenever I asked her, but she wasn't.

On the Friday of the first week back at school, Skylar raised her hand in history and asked, "Dr. McKenzie, is the Civil Rights Act of 1866 going to be on the test Monday?"

"Yes, of course." Connell whipped off her glasses to skim the study sheet she had just handed out. "I said all of chapter six."

"But you've never tested on anything you haven't discussed in class," said Skylar.

"We haven't done the Act of '66? That's right, we haven't."

Skylar persisted. "Can you talk about it on Monday? Postpone the test until Tuesday?"

Not just any Tuesday, but January 15, 1991, the Tuesday the world would stand still, holding its collective breath, all eyes turned toward the Middle East.

Connell hadn't mentioned the Persian Gulf crisis in class since our return from the holiday break. The omission was so obvious, Carlos had joked at lunch "Doc must've made a New Year's resolution not to mention the war."

Connell gazed out the window as if she were trying to see past the buildings of Orange Valley High, past the rotting citrus of the San Joaquin Valley, across vast countries and oceans—as if she were trying to see what was going on in the Middle East with her own eyes.

She turned toward us and said, "Um..."

Connell never said "um."

"Excuse me, class. I'm having difficulty concentrating these days. I imagine you are, too. Let's forget about tests for now. I'll give you an assignment instead. Today Congress will vote on whether it will authorize the president to send our country to war. To me, it looks like a real setup. Way back in November Bush told the whole world we're going to war January fifteenth, and he waits until now to see if it's okay with Congress. What can they say? Of course you can read about the outcome in the paper, but I want you to hear about it directly from your own congressman, Calvin Dooley. He will be conducting a town meeting at seven tomorrow evening at the College of the Sequoias lecture hall. You are all required to attend."

"Homework on a Saturday night? Ruthless!"

"It shouldn't take but an hour of your time," said Connell. "You can go out and have fun afterward."

"What's it cost?"

"Nothing, of course."

"I'm scheduled to work."

"Try to get off, but if you can't, you can't. If you attend the town meeting you will receive an extra-credit A that will bear as much weight as any test grade. If you cannot attend you will not be penalized, however, you must hand in a written excuse. For no attendance and no excuse you will receive an F."

"An extra-credit F, Doc?" asked Carlos.

Connell looked confused a moment, then smiled. "An extra-credit F, Carlos."

"Do we gotta do a report on it?"

"No report. I want you to listen to Congressman Dooley, not be scribbling in your notebooks."

"How will you know if we were really there?"

"I'll go down the roll on Monday. Just say yes or no. You can hand in your excuses at that time."

"We just tell you?" asked Carlos. "We could lie."

Connell gave the class one of her long, soulful looks. "You won't lie. I just know you won't."

***

"How's she going to know?" Carlos asked at lunch.

"She'll be there," said Scott. "Taking roll."

"I'll just tell her she must not have seen me."

"Oh, right." Lindsay fed Carlos a French fry. They had gotten together again at Winter Formal. I was trying to tolerate her just because we were in the same group, but I hardly thought of her as a friend anymore.

"McKenzie will trip you up with questions on Monday," said Skylar.

Carlos slumped and rolled his eyes upward. He fingered one of the silver peace earrings I was wearing. "What's with the Mercedes symbol? You're so crazy about our history teacher you wear advertisements for the car she drives?"

I jerked my head away. Scott glanced at the earrings and frowned. "I don't mind going to this town meeting thing. I could use an easy A from McKenzie."

"Well, I'm staying clear," said Roger. His inside information about Desert Shield always caused us to listen carefully to what he said about the impending war. "And you know what my excuse is going to be? I love my country. I'm not about to do anything un-American for an easy A."

Even Scott saw the fallacy of logic in this. "Attending a town meeting to hear how a congressman voted? Right, Dobbs, real un-American."

The tops of Roger's ears turned rosy, but he wouldn't give up. "It's got to be un-American if that commie teacher makes us do it."

I coughed and pressed my flattened palm against my chest. Eating lunch at the same table as Roger was bad for my digestion.

A whole bunch of us attended the town meeting together—Lindsay and Carlos, Skylar, Scott and me, and some other kids from AP History. We planned to go out for pizza afterward. The lecture hall at COS, which seats about two hundred, was packed. Walking down the aisle, I looked all around for Connell, but I didn't see her.

Congressman Calvin Dooley sat—or rather leaned—on a high stool, center stage. He had voted against going to war, siding with a small minority that was severely criticized by Bush, the rest of Congress, and many Americans.

A man in the audience confronted him about it. "You were elected to represent us in Congress. Clearly this community supports George Bush and his war effort. Then you turn around and vote however you please."

If Dooley felt backed against the wall, he certainly didn't show it. His arms hung relaxed at his sides, his shoulders slumped slightly forward. His eyes directly met his accuser's. In a calm, unwavering voice he explained that he was elected partly because of his constituents' trust in his moral judgment. He said, "I asked myself whether or not I could look a parent in the eye who had lost a son or daughter and say my vote backing military action was the best alternative available at the time. My answer was no."

Many other people raised their hands and were recognized. Nearly all of them spoke about the pending war, making it obvious whether they were in favor or opposed. The subject shifted to federal funding for freeze relief. It was hard to hear over the murmuring of the crowd and the squalls of a baby held in the arms of a woman sitting up front. She raised her thin, pale arm. "I want to know what you're doing about the deaths of our unborn children." Someone else asked about a national health care program.

Every question jumped to an entirely new topic, which made the discussion hard to follow, but the war came up again and again. A college-aged boy in back, waving an American flag so big it was hard to see how he got it through the door, shouted out, "I'm sick of war protesters. Our troops are fighting for something our country has always stood for—freedom. Anyone who doesn't want to support our troops under this flag can just leave the country."

A middle-aged man who said he was a Vietnam vet pleaded with Dooley. "Please do all in your power to stop this military action or you're going to be asking young people to make a sacrifice you can not even imagine."

I felt a hard, sudden jolt to my shoulder. Scott was on his feet. Tipping my head back, following my eyes up to him, was like trying to view the very top of a towering sequoia. I could see the black of his nostrils, the tensed muscles beneath his chin.

"I have an uncle and his name is Gary. He gave his all in Vietnam. He was caught by the Vietcong, imprisoned, and tortured. When he finally got home, war protesters met him at the airport." Scott's voice cracked and faltered. "Those people spit in my Uncle Gary's face. They called him 'baby killer.' We didn't support our troops in the last war, we've got to do it now, or else why would any man or woman bother to defend our country?"

Cheers and whistles broke out. Scott looked around, blinking, a tiny smile twitching at the corners of his mouth—a great orator sprung from the shoes of a shy, quiet boy. His chest puffed out. A gust of hot air pitched his voice over the restless crowd. "All war protesters are cowards and traitors. They lack the courage it takes to keep us free and strong, to keep the great and mighty USA number one."

The kids in our row leaped up in order, one by one, as if taking their turn in a wave. All around me people were bounding to their feet, reaching over my head to slap high fives with Scott, pat his back, or punch his arm.

The moderator called for order and soon after that the meeting was adjourned. My friends rose slowly, collecting purses and coats, leaning toward Scott to congratulate him. I turned away from him and pushed down the row, knocking Carlos back into his seat and stepping on Lindsay's foot.

"Hey, man, what's the rush?"

"Ow. Emily! Watch it."

I wove my way through the people in the aisle and made my way to the door. Outside the crowd turned into a mob. A band of people who had not attended the town meeting but seemed to have an instinct for trouble swarmed around the college. Car stereos erupted full blast, the bass notes shaking the ground. Beer bottles sailed over heads, thumped into bodies or shattered on the pavement. The guy with the big flag shouted, "This way for a pro-democracy rally." He and his friends began marching down the center of Mooney Boulevard. Drivers swerved to miss them, honking, swearing, and cheering. Other people stood in the beds of cruising pickup trucks waving flags and yellow ribbons and chanting, "Nuke Iraq! USA! Number one!"

I hurried down the sidewalk toward Main Street, looking straight ahead, fists clenched, making my way through a mob of people who simply weren't on my side. The cold night air seemed electrically charged by the friction of the opposition. No way was I really going to walk ten miles home, but I was mad enough to start out.

A low-riding car packed with young guys slowed and pulled close to the curb.

"Hey there, want a ride?"

I shook my head and kept moving. The boys whistled and shouted catcalls as they pulled out into traffic and sped ahead. It struck me that I had gotten off easy. The next carload of boys might be more persistent. They might get out of the car and come after me. They might not appreciate my peace earrings. I slipped them off and pushed them into my pocket.

I turned in at the next pay phone, called my mom, then loitered on the corner of Highway 63 and Main Street, all alone, waiting for her to come pick me up.

Dad showed up instead. When I got in the truck I could see he was pretty upset. "Scott let you wander off, all by yourself in the dark?"

"I don't think he noticed." I told my dad about Scott's little speech and all the people swarming around him. "He said all people against the war were traitors. He called *me* a traitor. I was so mad I just stalked out of there and kept walking."

Dad shook his head. "Emily, you know Mom and I don't usually agree when it comes to politics."

I nodded. Mom liked to joke that she went to the polls to cancel out Dad's vote. "I don't understand how you do it. Ever since this whole Persian Gulf thing came up in history class, Scott and I have sort of been on shaky ground."

"Try to look at the whole person, Emmie-Em." I know Dad was thinking of Scott standing by our family in the freezing cold, picking oranges. "Mommy says it's that new history teacher from back East that's got you all riled up. Outsiders don't much understand us valley people."

"You don't think it's good for a teacher to get her students thinking about the issues?"

"Sure, it's good, if it's really you doing your own thinking. Mom says this teacher has sort of got you brainwashed."

I frowned. "That's an exaggeration. I would say she's influential. Where is Mom anyway?"

"She's a little too far into the cabernet to be doing any driving tonight."

"Is Mom becoming an alcoholic?"

He laughed. "She is drinking more than usual, but it can be expected. People drink to ease their troubles. Give her a couple more weeks. She'll get over it."

"And the Hershey's Kisses?"

"A harmless vice, Emmie."

"Haven't you noticed? She's getting fat."

He laughed again but didn't say anything against her. If he thought she looked bad, he certainly wasn't going to admit it to me. At a year-end clearance sale she had bought herself three roomy pairs of sweats—gray, navy, and black—and these days that's all she could fit into.

At home, Mom had a cup of hot cocoa waiting—what she made for me when I was a little girl and got up in the middle of the night with a nightmare. It always soothed me back to sleep, even though chocolate is full of caffeine.

I settled in before the fire. Mom offered her candy to me. Her last bag of Kisses had been wrapped in green and red foil, and these were covered with silver and red for Valentine's Day. I took three silver ones and three red ones.

I unwrapped a silver one and sucked it thoughtfully. I told Mom all about the town meeting, then added, "I feel so alone in this. All my friends are against me, even Scott. *Especially* Scott. My own community! I always thought that Visalia was safe and friendly.

If I ever got into a bad situation, like car trouble, someone would be more than likely to help me out. But tonight I felt threatened."

I withdrew my earrings from my pocket and held them in my palm. The reflected fire made them glitter. "Walking home, I took these off and hid them. I was afraid if I got caught wearing them someone might hurt me. I felt the citizens of my own little safe hometown were ready to persecute me for my political beliefs. It's like my wanting peace is immoral, something dirty. It's like peace is a four-letter word."

Mom put her arm around my shoulders and held on tight. "Oh, my poor, darling girl; this is too much! You're studying the Civil War in history with that gruesome *Andersonville* with all those guys' legs and arms rotting off with gangrene. And your job is researching the Vietnam War with defenseless children charred black by napalm. And now this...this Desert Shield! It's too much for these narrow shoulders to bear. You cannot take responsibility for all the suffering in these wars! None of it is your fault!"

"But I can do my part to prevent this one. Do you know Cal Dooley voted against the war? His first vote in Congress! Wasn't that terribly brave of him? And if enough of us go out into the streets and show our disapproval, the president will have to see he's wrong. He's changed his mind before. He has to do what the people want. It's as simple as that."

"Oh, sweetheart, it's not simple. War is always very complicated. Why do you think he sent three hundred thousand troops to the godforsaken desert? They've dug in deep, they're ready to fight. Do you honestly think he's going to call them all home now?"

I shook my head. "Another Vietnam."

"Oh, it's not anything like Vietnam." Her hands cradled my elbows. "Do you realize Hussein has gassed his own people like Hitler did the Jews? Thousands of Kurds, whole villages lying dead in the streets. And all the weapons he's stockpiled—nasty stuff used in chemical and biological warfare. There's no telling the harm he can do if he's not stopped now and his weapons destroyed."

I shook her hands off me. "You're against me, too. So's Daddy."

"Oh, Emily!"

The phone rang, so close and loud I jumped.

"If it's Scott, tell him I was beaten and raped and left for dead."

Mom answered. "Hello? Yes. She's right here. I'll put her—you don't?"

"Well, I don't either," I snapped.

"Thanks for calling, Scott. Goodnight." Mom placed the receiver gently into its cradle. "He didn't know where you had run off to. He was extremely worried. He wanted to make sure you made it home okay. He's a very considerate young man. You're lucky to have him."

"Considerate?! He wouldn't talk to me, right?"

"Oh, Emmie, I hate to see you and Scott quarreling. You're so good together. He gets you to lighten up sometimes; he makes you happy. You know Daddy and I have never agreed on politics, but we agree on what's important—the basics."

"This *is* basic. Life or death; peace or war! I would be willing to respect Scott's opinion, but obviously he doesn't respect mine. You should have heard what he said about war protesters tonight."

"Don't let this lousy war tear you two apart. It's not worth it."

I sighed. Each time Scott and I fought over this, it seemed harder to patch things up. I was so tired I couldn't think straight. I deposited the remaining five Hershey's Kisses into the cellophane bag and pushed myself up. I said it again. "I feel so alone in this."

11

Connell. She was the first thing that sprang into my mind Sunday morning. Why hadn't I looked for her the previous evening? I had been so enraged by Scott's behavior I hadn't done the most obvious thing. She would have given me a ride home if only I had seen her. Now I couldn't wait to talk to her.

I jumped out of bed and pulled on jeans and a sweatshirt. To hell with the shower and makeup, I had to get to Connell. I ran a brush through my hair and hooked my peace earrings in my ears. I smiled at myself in the mirror and said, "Good morning, you wild and crazy peacenik."

I scooped up my research materials and ran down the stairs. In the kitchen, I guzzled a tall, frothy glass of orange juice. It was delicious. I thought, well, people will be drinking the few oranges we harvested this year instead of eating them—so what? They're still good for something.

Mom walked into the kitchen. "Hi, Emmie. Looks like you feel better this morning."

"Just great. Okay if I use the truck? I have to bring this stuff over to Connell's—I mean Dr. McKenzie's, and then there's the peace vigil."

"Isn't it a little early to be visiting people on a Sunday morning? What about church?"

"Can't make it this week. We've got lots of work to do." I kissed my mom and headed out.

It was hard not to speed on Highway 63. Several times I braked, knowing that the cops were out early with their radar guns. I fantasized talking with Connell about the previous night. Scott's emotional outburst, the fervor of the loud flag wavers, my fear of the noisy cruisers. In the morning light, it seemed so crazy, funny even, how upset I had been.

Connell and I would have a good laugh over it. I could just see her now, impersonating the whiny right-to-lifer with the fussy baby. I would mimic Scott's pro-war speech. God, I was so ready to be with someone who understood me.

I parked in Connell's apartment complex lot and ran up the stairs leading to her door. She was at the window over the sink, wearing a maroon silk bathrobe. The bathrobe should have clued me in—Connell's not the bathrobe type—and then she looked so surprised to see me. Maybe Mom was right—I was too early. But then she smiled and waved, and I was reminded about what my instincts had already told me: Connell would welcome me any time.

After what seemed like a very long time for her to get from the sink to the door, she answered. I burst in, still breathless from the stairs.

"Could you believe it? Those wild flag wavers. They were almost scary and—"

Connell's blank look caused me to stop. I stood there panting and waiting for some response.

"Oh! You mean the town meeting last night. How was it?"

"You weren't there?"

Connell looked down, tightening the sash of her robe. "No, Emily. Something came up. I—"

A man wearing nothing but socks and boxer shorts trotted out of her bedroom. "Oh, I thought I heard someone else's voice."

They were perfectly modest boxer shorts, fanning out at the waist and hitting him just above the knee. Even so, my hands flew up to my face, which had to be blazing magenta. I wanted the floor to open up and swallow me whole. "Oh! Oh! I'm such a retard! Sorry! Sorry!" I stepped backward, feeling behind me for the front doorknob.

"Wait, Emily." She turned to the man, her arms crossed in mock irritation. "For God's sake, Stuart, get your pants on so I can introduce you and Emily properly."

"Ah, so this is your little Emily." The "your" got to me. He extended his hand. My grip was weak, due to the fact that I had never shaken hands with a strange man wearing only underwear. "Stuart McKenzie. So very pleased to finally make your acquaintance, love." He talked with a slight British clip that reminded me of the old Beatles songs my mom sometimes played.

"Uh, me too," I stammered, trying to figure things out. He did say McKenzie, didn't he? Connell's husband? He was an inch shorter than she. A rosiness in his slightly curled-out ears and at the tip of his nose made him look younger, too, but then looks can be deceiving.

"Your pants, Stu." Connell gave him a smile—warm and familiar—the kind my mom gives my dad, especially when he is doing something stupid.

If they were married, why were they living apart? Were they separated and did they decide to get back together just last night? Or were they divorced and still old pals and occasional lovers?

Stuart walked back into the bedroom.

Connell extended her arm toward the kitchen table. "We were just going to have breakfast. Come join us."

"Oh, no, I couldn't. I feel terrible for barging in like this. For once I should have listened to my mom."

"Don't let it bother you, really. Stu's got to catch a plane in an hour."

"An hour! All the more reason why—"

"Nonsense, Emily. This is a chance for you two to get to know each other. Now, you toast the bagels while I grind the coffee beans."

Breakfast was all laid out when Stuart emerged again, this time dressed in a suit and tie. He glanced down at the table and exclaimed, "Lox! Tif, how thoughtful!"

"And not easy to find in this town. I must have tried five places. I know how much you love your lox."

He kissed her cheek as she bent over to pour the coffee.

"Tif? As in short for Tiffany?" I asked. "You don't really seem like a Tiffany to me." The only Tiffany I had ever known was a girl in my preschool who wore ringlets and big flouncy dresses and, at my fourth birthday party, peed down her leg into her black patent-leather Mary Janes.

"Awful, isn't it? When I was a little girl the neighbor's cocker spaniel was named Tiffany, too. Every time they called their dog, I would look up. I married Stu as an excuse to get rid of Tiffany."

"Ah, that's not the only reason, love."

Connell smiled. "There are a few other fringe benefits."

I thought about people calling me Rankin and decided I didn't like the idea, but Connell McKenzie sounded cool. Over breakfast I learned a lot about the McKenzies. They had met as grad students at Harvard working together in the Vietnam anti-war movement and had been married fourteen years. Stuart was not British but had had a British nanny, and Connell teased him about playing up his accent to sound cosmopolitan. Now Stuart was a corporate lawyer in Boston, specializing in what Connell called "hostile takeovers."

"Nothing's wrong with money," he said.

"Don't I know it," said Connell. I had expected her to say something about corporate America exploiting the poor.

I knew people often joked about things that bothered them the most, so I watched carefully for undercurrents of tension, but didn't see any. Still, it seemed that maybe over the years Stuart had become less socially conscious than Connell was.

From further talk I surmised that Stuart had quite a lot of money from his job, investments, and inheritance, while Connell had very little. I found out her car was a birthday present from him. They were married—why didn't they have the same amount of money? And why weren't they living together? They seemed to be happy that Stuart had managed an unscheduled overnight stop in Visalia on a business trip to San Francisco so soon after Connell had spent the two-week Christmas break with him in Boston. Certainly he had the means to support her while she wrote her book. It would save them the cost of this apartment in Visalia. Connell wouldn't have to teach high school and they could live together.

Stuart checked his watch. "About that time. I'll call a cab."

"Oh, that isn't necessary," said Connell. I figured, of course, she'd want to drive him to the airport, but in the next breath she added, "Take my car. Emily can swing me by to pick it up later."

"Oh, it's no imposition, Tif, you're sure? That would be great!" He seemed so grateful for the kind of courtesy my parents took for granted.

He got his overcoat and luggage from the bedroom. He kissed my cheek. "Nice to meet you, lovey. Take care of my girl, won't you? She's lonely out here in the Wild West."

He and Connell kissed. "Thanks for the surprise visit," she said. "All those flight changes seemed like a lot of bother."

"Well, I miss you."

"Me too, but Spring Break will be soon, huh?"

They both looked a little sad. Connell walked him to the car. Out the window, I could see her standing in the parking lot, her arms crossed, watching him drive out of sight.

When she came in, I must have had a funny look. "What?" she said.

"It's none of my business."

"Oh, Emily, I know what you're wondering. But once you've been married to a man for fourteen years you don't need to see him every day. I miss Stu, but he has his work and I have mine."

"I don't see that you like teaching high school very much, especially in Visalia. And you could write a book anywhere, like Boston, for instance."

"But how would I support myself? Stu and I don't believe in false dependencies. I wouldn't want a handout from him any more than he would want one from me. We signed a prenuptial agreement to that effect. It ensures our bond is not tainted by money. We are equal and free."

She didn't look all that free to me, but rather lonely and stuck in a place she didn't much like. "How much of your marriage have you spent together, if you don't mind me being nosey?"

"A good question." Connell cocked her head, thinking. "Easily more than two-thirds of the time. We'll be together again this summer."

"Don't you worry about his meeting someone else?"

"The bond between us will always be there, no matter who comes into our lives."

What did that mean—that it was okay for him to have girlfriends? And if so, couldn't one become more important to him than her? Couldn't she lose him altogether? If I want to have an important career, does that mean I'll have to sacrifice personal happiness? And what about kids? There didn't seem to be any place in Connell's scheme to have a family. In biology class, every life cycle we studied included reproduction. It seemed like not having kids meant living only half a life.

She touched my hand. "You're deep in thought."

"So many rules in your marriage! It would be like my mom drawing a salary from the Rankin Citrus Company."

Connell's eyes widened. "You mean she doesn't?"

At that point, I hated myself for dragging my mom into this, but I had to answer, "Well, no. It's her company, too."

"Oh, so if your parents divorce, the ranch would be sold and your parents would split the proceeds fifty-fifty?"

This conversation was making me uncomfortable, but since I had gotten into it, I had to find a way out. "I don't think so. That land has been in my dad's family four generations. Mom wouldn't expect it."

"So your father would buy your mother out? Pay her half in cash?"

I wasn't sure how much that would be, but it was in the millions. Not in cash, though—in land, trees, and machinery. "I don't know. I just know my dad would be fair to my mom."

Connell shook her head. "So your mother spends her life as a slave to your father, building up his company, and after a divorce she'd have nothing to show for it. You won't like hearing this, Emily, but I think you need to. Anytime a woman devotes herself to a man's career in the name of love, marriage, or whatever, she gets cheated. Your mother may be a very intelligent woman, but she's acting very foolish."

I tried to take another sip of my lukewarm coffee, but my hands shook and I set the heavy mug back down.

"I've upset you."

"It's okay."

"I'm sorry if you didn't like what I said about your mother. But you need to know how the world works. Obviously you're not going to learn it from her."

I sighed. "Let's just drop it."

"Okay. Let's talk about the town meeting instead." She stacked some of the dishes and shoved them aside. "What did you think about Cal Dooley? Start at the beginning and tell me everything that happened."

Was that what I was all excited about when I came barging in on Connell? The town meeting seemed to have happened weeks ago. It was hard to switch gears and conjure it all up for her. My mind kept drifting back to that sweet, cute man in boxer shorts with the British accent whom Connell hardly ever got to see.

***

I was still thinking about all this that evening when my mom came into my room to say goodnight. She kissed my cheek and smoothed my covers.

"Mom, what would happen if you and Dad got a divorce?"

"Oh, sweetie, that's not going to happen." She hugged me, tears surfacing—tears that came easily for her these days. I sometimes caught her staring out the kitchen window at all the rotten fruit, tears streaking her cheeks. "We're going through bad times now, sure. Daddy and I may snap at each other once in a while or even yell, but we're not about to—"

"I know, I know. I'm just asking what if? When you got married did you consider getting a prenuptial agreement? You know, arrange your finances a certain way?"

Mom sank to the bed. "Emily, what's this all about?"

I didn't dare mention Connell's name. I said, "Oh, it just came up in history. We're studying the Nineteenth Amendment—women's rights and all. This girl was saying the only way marriage is fair to women is if there's a prenuptial agreement in case of divorce."

"Daddy would be fair to me."

"Even if you hated each other's guts?"

"Emily! I can't imagine. Daddy and I would be civil toward one another no matter what."

"Even if he married some hot young girl a few years older than me?"

Mom just laughed at that. "I haven't noticed any hot young girls cruising by our sofa lately."

"That's not funny, Mom."

"No? Well, I guess I can joke about it because I know it's not as serious as it looks to you."

"Yes, it is. Daddy doesn't even go into Sanger to breakfast with the ranchers anymore."

"I guess misery doesn't always love company. At least not in your dad's case. He does the morning chores. He's getting a small crew together to strip the trees. He'll be out there overseeing the job, you'll see. Give him time, Emily. He's suffered a blow."

"What about the money part, of divorce, I mean? I'm just wondering, you know, for my class. What would happen if you got a divorce?"

"I don't know. I never thought about it." Mom glanced down at the newly acquired roll of fat around her middle. "I'm actually not enjoying this conversation very much."

"Would Daddy sell the company and divide the money fifty-fifty?"

"Of course not. I wouldn't want him to. He'd be certain we had a nice place to live, child support, college tuition for you kids."

"Yeah, but what about you?"

"I'm not helpless, you know. Although I don't imagine my old English lit degree would get me very far in today's job market, I could take some computer courses or something. I would expect Daddy to support me until I was retrained and found a decent job, but then I would want to be independent as soon as possible."

"That's all? That's your big reward for slaving away in the Rankin Citrus Company the last twenty years?"

"Oh, Emily, I haven't been slaving. I've been having a wonderful life."

"So you think those prenuptial things are bad?"

"No. I guess they're good for some people. Like when a man and a woman both want to go to college, but the couple can only afford to send the guy, and he becomes a doctor or something, then wants a divorce. Well, then I think he owes his ex-wife an education."

"How comes it's always the guy who gets to go to college first?"

"That's a very good question." She fluffed my bangs. "Anyway, don't worry, Emmie-Em. Daddy and I aren't getting a divorce."

"History class, remember, Mom?"

"Well, we're not." Mom switched off the light as she left my room.

I lay there in the dark thinking that this whole subject made me feel like a weakling. I didn't think I could stand it living alone like Connell. Mom seemed happy enough, but only because she liked her duties as a rancher's wife. I wanted to live with my husband and not have to keep his books.

I tried to imagine being married to Scott. If I told him I had to spend a week in Washington, DC, would he have a fit? I thought he might. What does an ex–high school athlete do for a living anyway? Major in business and open a trophy shop downtown, a small operation where his wife keeps the books?

I groaned and rolled over. And over.

It wasn't easy falling asleep that night.

12

Scott clutched the ball, inside and low, and ran, the fastest man in a fast break. He launched it toward the basket, the shot a smooth, clear-sailing arc. Whoosh—that sweet sound.

Scott averaged twenty-six points a game, but Redwood, the team we were playing, had a great defense. The score was 74-70. The shouts of Orange Valley fans reverberated around the gym, accompanied by the squeaks of shoes and the rhythmic boom-boom of the ball.

"Lockhart! Lockhart! He's our man."

My man, even though lately we seemed more without each other than with. It was Wednesday afternoon, and we had patched things up over the phone on Sunday night. He insisted he was defending his Uncle Gary's honor, not speaking out against me. "I wasn't even thinking of you as a protester," he said. "So you stood on Mooney Boulevard a couple of times to show you don't want us to go to war in the Persian Gulf. That's different; you're not hard-core. I was talking about the protesters who spit on my uncle when he returned from Vietnam. Some thanks they gave him for serving his country, for wrecking his life."

I could see Scott's point. I wished I had never heard of the damn Persian Gulf. Nineteen hours had passed since the stroke of midnight, Eastern Standard Time, January 15. The night before on CNN, Bernard Shaw had said, "Personally, I do not think there will be a war." Oh, if only that were true!

Scott got the ball again, his foot in the paint, his back to the basket. He faked a low pass to Carlos, then leaped up, spun a 360, and slam-dunked mid-turn. It was a flashy move, like he was showing off, but he wasn't, not Scott. He was just playing his game.

My Scott was a local hero. People loved to tell him basketball was his ticket out of the valley, his way to fame and fortune. They'd slap him on the back and say, "NBA boy, I'm going to be able to say I knew you when." Scott would smile his shy smile and shrug. He knew playing pro ball was one chance in a million. Maybe his game would take him to college, a good college like UCLA, but what then? He once told me, "I've got some God-given talent and the right body type, the least I can do is work at it." His game took him to his next shot, and he didn't think much beyond that.

Scott approached the basket again. He extended his long, lanky arm, the ball held firmly in one gigantic hand. And then his wrist made its loose, graceful move. Whoosh! I had seen that same gorgeous wrist pluck an orange in a dark, deserted grove on the coldest night of the year. So what if Scott was pro-war and I was for peace? He was still a good guy.

76-70. "Lockhart! Lockhart! He's our man."

"Come on, Emily," said our squad leader, Yesenia. "Let's build the pyramid for Scott."

I nodded at her and leaped onto the mini-tramp. Lindsay, Donna, and Amy took their kneeling positions.

"See that basket, see that rim!"

Vanessa and Jamie built the second story.

"See how Lockhart dunks it in."

"Your attention, please!" It was the voice of our principal, Mrs. Cisneros, coming to us over the intercom. The seriousness of her tone caused a hush to fall over the gym. "An attack over Baghdad is underway. The war has begun."

There was a beat of silence, and then wild cheers erupted from the bleachers. Spectators threw cups and paper containers. Someone shouted, "Go USA!"

My knees turned to Jell-O. A rock of fear felt heavy in my stomach. So, it's really happening. My efforts did nothing to stop it. How many people are already dead, how many more would die? Were there women and children beneath piles of rubble? I turned to the people laughing and shouting and hugging. It felt like a nightmare—something horrifying was happening to me, yet no one around me seemed to notice how terrible it was.

"Em-mul-lee! Hurry it up!" Lindsay whined. She was still kneeling at the base of the unfinished pyramid. Already Skylar had climbed up to stand on Vanessa's and Jamie's backs. On the wings of the structure was Sharon, her thigh lunged, waiting to receive me. By now I should be through my flip and handspring, but I had not left the mini-tramp.

My bounce got slower, lower.

"Go, Emily, go!" someone shouted from the bleachers. "This one is for our troops!"

A chant rose up. "USA! Number One! USA! Number One!"

I leaped off the mini-tramp and launched into a flip, landing on my feet. I extended my hands over my head for the handspring.

"Nuke Iraq! Nuke Iraq!"

I froze, my eyes fixed on the pyramid, now starting to sway.

"Get moving, Emily." Coach Metz's voice was low and threatening. "Skip the handspring and mount—now!"

I stared at the pleading faces of my squad like they were behind glass and I couldn't reach them. Skylar wavered, then dropped to her bottom. Vanessa's knee slipped off of Lindsay's back. The whole pyramid collapsed into a heap of six writhing bodies. Lindsay clutched her ankle and howled.

I started walking, the big green exit sign looming ahead over the door. I just had to make it that far. Hisses and boos rose up from the crowd. As I swung open the door, sticky liquid and ice hit me square in the back. I kept walking as if I didn't feel a thing.

At home my parents and I sat glued to the TV. In between live coverage, CNN played the tape of the initial attack over and over. Their reporters—Bernard Shaw, John Holliman, and Peter Arnett—were holed up in a room on the ninth floor of the Al Rasheed Hotel in downtown Baghdad.

"Something is happening outside," said Shaw. "We're getting starbursts...in the black sky."

"They're coming over our hotel. You can hear the bombs now," said Arnett.

Holliman broke in, "We just heard—whoa! Holy cow! That was a large airburst that we saw."

"God!" I couldn't believe it. "Aren't they afraid? What's to stop them from getting hit, too?"

"I guess we're not aiming for the hotel," said Mom.

"It could still get hit," said Dad. "Friendly fire."

I hated those euphemisms the military thought up—cutesy names for unspeakable horrors. "Friendly fire" sounded like something you gathered around to toast marshmallows and sing "Blowing in the Wind."

The TV showed what looked like an extravaganza of Fourth of July fireworks when actually it was Baghdad getting bombed, buildings and bridges blowing up, people dying in the flashes of light.

Ryan sauntered out of his room, dazed by a long session of Nintendo. "Hey, Mom, when's dinner? I'm starving."

"It's coming," she said, leaning toward the TV and waving him away. She hadn't bothered cooking and had ordered pizza instead.

On the TV a fighter jet pilot was being interviewed in his cockpit filled with dozens of meters and gadgets. The scene switched to a few men loading three-foot bombs onto the jet. There was footage of a building centered in the target. Then the building flew apart.

"Cool!" exclaimed Ryan. "What show is this?"

"It's not a show," I said. "It's the war." Desert Storm—the first armchair war in history.

The scene switched again to bombs exploding in the night over Baghdad.

"Which war? What's the name of the movie?"

"This is a newscast. This is really happening, right now!"

Ryan's eyes widened. He ran to the sliding glass door and flung aside the drapes.

"You lie! There's no bombs going off out there."

"Not here, Ryan," I said. "It's clear over in Iraq, halfway around the world."

"I heard of Iraq! My teacher says we might go to war with them. When will they start bombing us? When will the war get to our house?"

Mom laughed. "Never. Somehow the wars that the US fights in never do make it to our house."

Ryan swung his fist in the air. "Shoot. You mean we're having a war and I'm going to miss the whole thing?"

"Be thankful," said Dad, pulling Ryan onto his knee. "War is no fun."

We watched needle-nosed fighter jets coming in for a landing. One pilot interviewed by the newsman reported that they had hit all their targets and all the planes that had been sent out had returned safely.

There was a lot of back slapping and arm socking, and the men were jumping up and down, happy to be alive. Some guys drew hearts and their girlfriends' names on the bombs that were about to be loaded onto jets. When interviewed, the servicemen seemed to swagger while standing still.

One soldier said, "I've never been fired on and I'd like to know what it's like. I want to know if I can stand up to it." General Schwarzkopf came on the screen looking something like the Pillsbury Doughboy in fatigues, squinting into the camera and talking tough. Other soldiers were rolling over the desert in huge tanks, defusing mines with no apparent damage to themselves.

"It is *too* fun!" Ryan pointed at the screen. "Look, those guys are having lots of fun."

Right, I thought, they're loving it—the adventure of their lives. The danger was part of the thrill, although there didn't seem to be very much danger for the US so far. Where else but war would you get to drive a multimillion-dollar jet or tank? Life-sized GI Joe toys. No wonder the guys in my class were so gung ho. They wished they could be there themselves, not to free Kuwait, especially, but just for the sheer adventure. It sure beats the hell out of the Visalia Mall.

The phone rang.

"I'll get it," Mom said, reluctantly getting up. "It doesn't look like pizza is going to make it. Everyone probably had the same idea. I'll fix some sandwiches."

Mom returned from the kitchen too soon and empty-handed. She turned the sound down on the TV. "Emily, I want to hear it from you. What happened at the game?"

My heart began to race. "We won—I guess."

"That was Coach Metz on the phone. She wants you in her office before the first bell. Lindsay has torn ligaments in her ankle and Coach is holding you responsible."

I told my parents the whole story. "Don't you see? We started the cheer for Scott and it ended up being for death and destruction. All those people seemed so happy that hundreds of thousands of people are going to get killed. It paralyzed me. I couldn't make myself be a part of it."

"I understand how you feel," said Mom, "but sometimes you just have to go along with the program, do what's expected of you. Your friend is suffering due to your negligence."

"Oh, don't worry about Lindsay. Whatever physical pain this causes her will be made up by all the attention she gets." I mimicked Lindsay's high-pitched, whiny voice. "Carlos, be a sweetie and take my books. Oh, Roger, thank you for getting the door. Oh, Scott, see what that bad ol' Emily has done to me? Carry me into the classroom, would you, Scottie?"

Ryan laughed but my parents remained stern.

I crossed my arms. "If someone had to get hurt, I'm glad it was Lindsay."

"Some pacifist you turned out to be," said Dad.

That made me ashamed. I tried to feel a little sorry for Lindsay. Torn ligaments were killers—she'd be black and blue to her knee—but the image I had created of Scott carrying her into history class like a bride over the threshold was just too vivid. I searched deep inside me for remorse—all the way back into the recesses of my earliest memories of our shared childhood—and still I was spitefully glad.

"Go call Lindsay and apologize," said Mom.

"I can't do that. It wouldn't be sincere."

***

I sat in the chair in Coach Metz's office as she paced back and forth in front of me. She'd lectured me for five minutes and was now repeating the high points. "The squad trusted you. They believed you would follow through with your part of the pyramid no matter what. That trust is going to be hard to win back. What have you to say for yourself?"

"It was a freak coincidence, Coach. It could never happen the same way. Never. People were shouting about nuking Iraq. I wasn't going to do a cheer for killing people."

"This isn't about politics, Emily. It's about responsibility to your team. You may think you have the rights of an individual, but as a team member you don't. The safety of your team comes first. Just remember, you're dispensable like everyone else. I could replace you just like that." She snapped her fingers before my face. "Now, I'm going to give you some time to think about this. You're suspended from the squad for two weeks."

The suspension hit hard, like I'd been slapped. I expected just a scolding. I thought about what I would miss: two home games and a trip to LA that I was looking forward to. Worse than that, my pride was crushed. Coach Metz and I had never been close, but I thought she appreciated me. I thought she respected me for how hard I worked for the squad. Now she was saying I didn't count for anything.

Beyond her shoulder I could see the tallest trophy in her case. It was from last year's AACC Championships, first place in the Girls' Stunt Division. I'd like to see her win that one this year without me.

I imagined Connell standing behind Coach, smiling back at me. "I heard what you did at the game yesterday," she'd say to me. "You're a brave girl, Emily. Most everyone else would have buckled under peer pressure, gone with the flow, but you stood up for what you believe in. I'm proud of you."

I glared at the top of Coach's head as she bent over the paperwork. I gripped the arms of the chair tighter to keep from shaking with anger. She tore off one of the triplicate copies and extended it across her desk. I just looked at it. She shook it impatiently. "Here. Take this home, have it signed by your parents, and return—"

"I quit!" I leaped up and ran down the hall toward Connell's classroom, bearing the news of my resignation from the cheerleading squad like a cat laying a dead mouse at her mistress's feet.

13

It turned out I didn't really feel like seeing Connell. I knew what she'd say about cheerleading being sexist and all that, and I wasn't in the mood to hear it. I decided to hold a vigil at Scott's locker instead. I stood there looking at the floor, wishing I were invisible. When kids or teachers passed me, I only saw as high up as their knees. If I knew them, I didn't know it. People left me alone.

At last I heard Scott's loping stride. I looked up. His face was still pink from his shower, and he was laughing with the guys. When he saw me his whole body sagged and his face closed over. His friends fell away without a word.

He said hi but he didn't touch me. He acted like spinning his combination lock was the most important thing in the world.

"I need to talk to you," I said, the words raspy in my throat.

"So talk."

"Not here. Not at school. Will you still give me a ride home today?"

"What do you mean 'still'?" The door of his locker flew open. He stopped his stuff from falling out with his broad palm. With his other hand he rummaged beneath sweats, stale sack lunches, and loose papers for the books and notebooks he needed for his morning classes.

"I mean, after..." I pictured the faces of my teammates floating over the collapsing pyramid. "Hold me."

"God, Emily, hang on a sec." He dug faster. He stuck a notebook under his chin, clenched his heavy history book between his knees, then pawed through his locker some more.

I stood there crying and waiting and thinking if he really loved me he would have let the whole mess tumble across the hall as he swept me into his arms. Finally, when he had what he needed, he slammed the locker shut and placed the stack of books at his feet. Only then did he move toward me. And still, he wasn't exactly hugging me. His arms across my shoulders felt suspended, tense. I leaned into him, clung to his waist, pressed the side of my face against his chest. My ear was over his heart—I could hear it racing.

"Pulse is up," I said.

Only then did he really hold me. I don't know how much time passed. It felt short; it also seemed too long. Traffic was picking up in the hall. I pushed away. On his T-shirt was an imprint of my lashes in runny mascara. It looked like the silhouette of an injured butterfly.

***

I timed my entrance into history so that I was too late to have a private conversation with Connell and too early to come face to face with Lindsay. I still wasn't ready to apologize to her—it felt like I never would be. I stared straight down at my notebook, ignoring my classmates' rude remarks and teasing.

Then, just after the bell, I heard the heavy stomps of a single foot, a high-pitched "Waaugh," and wooden crutches clattering against the metal legs of a desk.

"Hey, Carlos, you do that to her?"

"Yeah."

"Tough guy."

"Damn straight. If my woman gets out of line, that's what she gets." Carlos crossed his arms over his chest, posturing, and the whole class cracked up.

"It was Emily," said Donna. "You know it was Emily who did it."

"Yeah, Rankin. Staging a war protest in the middle of a game."

"What happened?"

"Didn't you see it? The whole pyramid went crashing down on poor Lindsay's ankle."

"That's enough," said Connell. "Lindsay, turn around in your seat and stop talking."

"I wasn't talking."

"She wasn't talking."

"Dr. McKenzie, may I please rest my foot on a seat?" asked Lindsay. "Some of my ligaments got sort of torn."

"Of course, Lindsay. It's not the sort of thing for which one asks permission, unless one wants to attract attention to oneself."

"Hey, Doc, stop picking on Lindsay."

"Yeah, just because it was teacher's pet that did it to her."

Connell let that one slide. She got right down to business, lecturing on the Reconstruction Acts and Johnson's impeachment. It was a lot of material to cover in one period, and she spoke and scrawled like mad to get it all in. The kids were bent over their notebooks, hurrying to get it down. I think we were all surprised we had to work that hard. We expected she'd spend most of the period discussing the war, but she didn't even mention it.

I collected my stuff before the bell, and when it rang I bolted. I forgot about Lindsay's leg sticking out into the aisle and nearly tripped over it. Just at the last minute, I managed a little hop, stumbled several steps, and caught myself, bracing against the wall.

Lindsay's squeal hit me square between the shoulder blades. "Hey. Just 'cause you're not sorry doesn't mean you have to hurt me again."

At lunch, I did the cowardly thing once more, hiding out in the library with my M&M's. That was the worst of it, and eventually the school day was over.

***

I met Scott in the parking lot and we drove, hardly speaking. I waited until we were on the ranch, walking hand in hand through the orange groves. Stripping had begun but there was no hurry, and plenty of rotting fruit hung heavy on the trees. It was as still as a cemetery.

"I quit."

"What do you mean? You quit the squad?"

"Uh-huh. Coach Metz hit me with a two-week suspension, so I got mad and quit."

"Wow. Was it a pride thing?"

"Uh-huh."

Scott raised his eyebrows, his sleepy eyelid inching upward. "It's probably not too late to go crawling back."

"I don't feel like crawling back, although, I have to admit, I'm beginning to regret it."

Scott shook his head. "This is gonna hurt you, Emmie."

"It actually felt great. You should have seen the look on Coach's face. Let's see her win the stunt title without me."

"Doesn't make a damn bit of difference to her. Coaches are always gonna sacrifice the individual for the team. I bet it's the hardest thing they learn but they learn it best. A guy gets to thinking he's better than everyone else and he makes a mistake, maybe a couple, hurts his team somehow, and he's out. I've seen it happen every year of my game, and I'm talking since third grade. I've slipped up a couple of times myself and had to take a tongue lashing, then swallow my pride, but every time the coach was right. The team is what counts—always."

"But, Scottie, in this situation—"

"No situation is any different."

"Did you hear those bloodthirsty people? They were all 'Nuke Iraq.' I'm not obligated to cheer for killing."

"I'll admit it was weird, the timing of that announcement, but still, you let your team down. Now you're going to miss it, Em. It's no fun going through life without them. Now what are you going to do in your spare time?"

"Oh, I don't care. Cheerleading is sexist and stupid anyway. I don't want to do it anymore."

"Bullshit."

"It keeps women down."

"That's McKenzie filling your head. That's her talking."

I sighed. "Maybe yes, maybe no."

"And it was her that got you all fired up, going off to war protests."

I stepped in front of him and shoved him in the chest. "Don't! Just don't, okay? She never even asked me to go to those peace things. If you don't believe I'm a pacifist deep down in my heart, then you don't know me. And if you don't know me, then why do you—"

"I believe you, Emmie." He was quiet and calm. "I'm just saying she was the one who gave you the idea."

"So what? Teachers are supposed to make you think."

"I don't see where it's done any good. Did your prancing up and down Mooney stop the war from happening? You and I seem to have been fighting ever since McKenzie hit town, and now, all of a sudden, you aren't a cheerleader anymore."

"Scott, in my heart it's done some good. Something's changed in me. If more people changed like this, if most people did, there'd be no more wars."

"Oh right! You think you're living in a fairy tale?"

"The Berlin Wall!" I flung my arms out to my sides and let them slap down against my thighs. "Poof—it's gone. Not a single shot fired. People naturally want their freedom. They'll get it."

"Great! So now West Germany is overpopulated. Big deal."

I turned and walked away from him.

He caught up with me in two strides, put his arm around me, and pulled me close. "You know you can't walk away from a guy whose legs are twice as long as yours."

"Very funny," I said, but I let him kiss me anyway.

"Emmie, I feel bad about the war, too. I don't want people getting killed any more than you do."

"Sure. American people."

"Iraqis too. I'd like just one of them dead. Sa-Dam."

"Oh, don't say it like George Bush. To think we have a president who doesn't even understand simple diplomacy. We're all going to pay for that single mispronunciation, big time. It makes me sick."

"Well, all of it makes me sick. I wasn't cheering with the rest of those maniacs at the game. My stomach turned over."

"Somehow, though, you struggled through to win the game."

"Of course I finished the game. And you should have finished the pyramid. But it's done now. Forget it. At least you nailed the right person."

"What? Your Winter Formal date? Your Snow Queen? The woman of your dreams?"

He groaned. "Can we forget that? That act she put on in history...I wanted to stomp on her ankle myself."

That made me laugh, the thought of my big Scottie purposely hurting anyone.

"I'm just curious. Does Carlos care anything about her?" I asked.

"Are you kidding? He's gone on her! Been that way since seventh grade."

"Did Carlos say anything about me?"

"Nope."

"Does he hate me?"

Scott shook his head. "He doesn't blame you. It was an accident. It will blow over."

"She'll be on crutches a while. She's not going to let me forget it soon."

He sighed. "Lindsay's just being Lindsay. So what?"

"Well, she turned your head."

"Naw, that was only 'cause I was so pissed at you."

"She turned your head."

"Rotten personality. Nice ass."

"What?!" I ducked out from under his arm, ran to the nearest tree, and plucked an orange. It had thawed and was soft and squishy with a big green spot of mold. I spun around and fired it at him. It landed splat in the middle of his chest.

His eyes popped and he started to sputter. "You...you...pacifist! This means war!" He bent down and reached for one of the really rank oranges that had been rotting on the ground.

"No fair, no fair. You've got to at least pick them." I sprinted toward the house, laughing so hard I was doubling over. He closed in on me fast and got me in the butt. The sting wasn't nearly as bad as the stink. I spun and reached high for another orange. He got me on the thigh, this time with more solid ammunition—more punch, less smell. I threw without aiming and missed. He got another direct hit on my shoulder. I saw four oranges in the palm of his broad hand—it was like looking down the barrel of a semi-automatic.

I clasped my hands over my head and crumpled to my knees. "Truce! Truce!"

Another orange hit me on the elbow. "Scottie, be nice."

Then he was right on top of me. I squeezed my eyes shut. I heard his ammunition drop at my knees with a hollow thud. I looked up. He wiped his hands on his jeans and pulled me up. I felt the stone of my little green promise ring press into his fingers as he squeezed my hand. "I feel like kissing you, but you stink too bad."

"Well, so do you."

"I love you."

When we kissed I thought this is it, this is how it's supposed to be. At last things were right between us. I wanted Scott and only Scott. He broke apart from me, looked into my eyes.

"I want you—"

"I was thinking the same thing."

"—to crawl back."

"Oh, that. Scottie, I can't. I—"

He shook me gently. "Hear me out, babe. You know there's lots of road trips at the end of the season. I want you beside me on that bus. I don't want you missing out on the fun either. Go talk to Coach. It'll be worth it, you'll see."

I knew he was probably right, but it didn't seem to change anything inside of me. "I want to. I just don't think I can."

"Try, Emily. Try hard."

14

"Emily! Will you please stop pacing?" Mom dumped chicken pieces into a paper sack, causing a cloud of flour to billow out. "I know you're upset, but give the linoleum a break. I don't think we can afford to replace it soon."

It was late Saturday afternoon and I was helping Mom fix dinner. Besides the country fried chicken, we were having mashed potatoes, creamed onions, and deep-dish apple pie—"comfort food," my Mom called it. I guess she thought I needed it because at that moment the basketball team and cheerleading squad were in LA without me.

Mom handed me a bowl of small white boiling onions and a paring knife. "Here, cry in the onions."

"I don't feel like crying," I said. But I settled down at the kitchen table anyway and began chopping off the ends of the onions. I was still too mad at Coach Metz to care about not being on the LA trip. Still, it felt lonely knowing Scott and all my friends were out of town having fun, and here I was, cheated out of my Saturday-night date. The rest of the week loomed ahead, empty and dismal. And then there was the war. I sighed. "I just don't know what to do."

"Talk to her. Coach Metz might act really strict with you girls, but she's a reasonable person."

"Mom, could you forget about the small stuff for a while and look at the big picture?"

"Oh, the war, you mean."

I nodded. "I'm wondering about the peace vigil tomorrow. I don't think I should go anymore. The situation has changed. Before, I was trying to stop our country from going to war, and now that it has, well, it isn't exactly being a traitor, but isn't it demoralizing for our troops?"

"We 'Nam protesters were accused of being traitors, and it hurt a lot. I love my country, but I felt our government was making a big mistake over there."

"Shouldn't I accept what the majority rules? Isn't that the whole idea of a democracy? Like Cal Dooley." After being defeated in voting against the war, he, along with the rest of Congress, voted in favor of a resolution that offered full support to our troops.

"Dooley is in a different situation," said Mom. "If Congress rebelled against the president on this then our government looks weak to the outside world. If an ordinary citizen rebels, then it's just freedom of speech."

"Maybe if war protests continue, pressure will be on Bush to make the war as short as possible."

"Maybe."

"At least some lives will be saved."

"Maybe not."

I turned to look at her. "What do you mean?"

"Sometimes the most carnage happens after a war. As soon as the US leaves the Gulf, those Iraqis that opposed Hussein are going to have hell to pay."

"But if we win the war, like it looks like we're going to, won't Hussein be thrown out of power?"

"Our job is to drive him out of Kuwait. That's all."

"But won't his own people get so mad at him for getting in a war he couldn't win—all those people killed, his country torn up—that someone would rise up and seize power?"

"There's too many factions in Iraq. And none of their leaders seem to be strong enough to stand up against Hussein."

"My God, this is complicated." I covered my eyes with my hands "Ow!" I screamed, forgetting the onion juice on my fingers.

Mom guided me to the sink and helped me rinse my eyes with cold water. "Honestly, Em. I just hope you survive the war."

***

Sunday morning I still didn't feel right about attending the peace vigil. If Connell asked why I wasn't there, I would just tell her how I felt. If she disapproved—tough. Certainly she would understand I had to follow my own conscience in this.

I attended church with my family, and afterward we went to an all-you-can-eat breakfast bar for more comfort food. At this rate my family would make it through the freeze and the war only to die of heart disease.

Back home, I tried to settle down to studying, but I couldn't concentrate. I started pacing in my room, noticed the path already beaten in my rug, and went for a jog in the orange groves. After a shower, I called Scott to see if he was up for a bike ride or something. His Mom said he wasn't home—he and Carlos had gone off somewhere. This hurt. He'd been gone almost the whole weekend, and I figured he would have at least called before making plans without me.

After I hung up, I went to Mom begging for the keys to the pickup.

"Where to, Emmie-Em?"

"I don't know. I just have to get out of here. Can't I just drive?"

"You know that's not allowed."

"Just this once? I'll report back in an hour." I took the keys off their hook and dangled them hopefully.

Her mouth tightened. "Wear your seat belt."

"I always do." I kissed her cheek. "I'll call."

I was free to go anywhere. I could head east up to Three Rivers or north to Fresno. But at the intersection of 63, the truck turned south toward town. I guess my instincts were guiding it.

In Visalia the truck headed toward church. I don't remember ever going to church two times in one day, but I didn't feel extra holy doing it. I was just hoping that sitting in the dark, cool, empty church I'd be closer to God, that He'd somehow hear my prayers better.

Dear God, can't You be reasonable about this? Can't You shake some sense into Hussein and Bush? Although they call You by different names, they both seem to believe You are on their side. That can't be right. You can't want them to be killing each other's people. Maybe they just believe what they want to believe and don't pay attention to You at all. So, if You can't get through to the leaders, could You go to work on the soldiers? Help them to throw down their weapons, one side or the other, or all at once. I don't care which, just get this war over quickly. Amen.

I started to rise, then felt a tinge of guilt, like I hadn't completely leveled with God or myself. I added,

Well, actually God, I do care. I'd like it to be the Iraqis who surrender—if You don't mind. Amen again.

I started to leave once more, then sunk to my knees.

It's not that I think Americans are better than Iraqis—I don't. I don't even think they have any business interfering with Middle Eastern affairs. But if you let the Americans win, well, then maybe they won't go to war again real soon. You know, Americans are real sore losers. They still feel awful about screwing up in Vietnam and they aren't going to be happy until they win big. Don't get me wrong, I'm not running down my countrymen. I don't think Americans are any worse than...oh, I give up! Sorry, God, this isn't coming out right. Amen. And peace.

Leaving the church, I didn't feel any better; I felt ridiculous. Why should God bother listening to me when I didn't even make sense to myself?

Next I decided to cruise by Recreation Park, see if I could spot Scott and Carlos shooting hoops. If they were there, I didn't plan on stopping—I didn't want Scott to think I needed to always be hanging around him like some girls act with their boyfriends. I just had a strong urge to rake my eyes over him.

I turned down Jacob Street and scanned the basketball courts. Deserted. I didn't know what to do with myself next. I didn't feel like dropping by Skylar's and I didn't want to go to the mall, but I wasn't ready to go home either. At Main, I turned down Mooney, deciding to drive by the peace vigil, just to see who had shown up.

Nearing Walnut, I got into the left lane, planning to make a U-turn and head for home right after I took a quick look. A red light gave me plenty of time to check things out. The peaceniks looked about the same except there were a few more than usual. I spotted some familiar faces, including Connell's and Elena's. A new development was a small opposing group gathered in front of the car wash on the east side of Mooney.

The pro-war crowd was small but loud. They honked horns, jeered at the protesters, clanked beer cans and bottles, and chanted "USA! Number One!" Someone dressed in a red-and-white-striped top hat and pants and a blue star-spangled jacket was fake-punching a guy dressed in a robe and a turban. The Iraqi character cowered defenselessly, rolling his big brown eyes in mock terror at the Uncle Sam character.

I knew those eyes—the thick lashes were a giveaway, even from across the street. Then I noticed Uncle Sam's legs were exceptionally long, his ankles sticking out of his striped pants. I hit the steering wheel with the heel of my hand. "Damn them," I said aloud.

The light changed. I took the U-turn fast, veered into the car wash parking lot, and braked hard. I marched up to Scott, my arms crossed. "Scott Lockhart, of all the despicable, crude, uncouth—I wouldn't believe it if I wasn't seeing it with my own eyes."

"Believe it, baby." Carlos touched his forehead, nose, chin, and bowed deeply.

"Oh, shut up, I'm not talking to you! Scott, how could you?"

"It's a nasty job, but someone's got to support our troops. Sorry you don't approve." His eyes turned flat and mean. His smile was more like a sneer. He tipped his top hat at me.

I twisted off the little green promise ring and slam dunked it into the hat. It bounced against the cheap plastic, then landed with a final clink.

I don't remember getting back into the truck, pulling out into traffic, and U-turning again to park on the opposite side of the street. In my next conscious moment I was yanking a peace sign out of Elena's hands, muttering, "I need to borrow this." I glared across the street at Scott, who paid no attention to me as he and Carlos continued their distasteful charade.

Then the rational and the irrational had a private little war inside of me.

Irrational: I hate him for doing this.

Rational: That's your Scottie.

Irrational: I never loved him, not really. How could I love anyone so insensitive?

Rational: Calm down. You're just upset. You don't really want to break up with him.

Irrational: I don't ever want to speak to him again. He's totally against me.

Rational: How can you think that? Didn't you turn to him when you quit the squad and didn't he comfort you? Didn't you have a heart-to-heart talk with him about the war, agreeing to disagree? Didn't he stand by you and your family picking oranges on the coldest, darkest night of your life? That's it! That's it! That's why I'm so angry! In private, Scott is sweet, gentle, and understanding; it's in public that he attacks my principles—at the town meeting and now—in the most disgusting ways.

Irrational: It's not just my beliefs, it's me personally. Peace can't be separate from me unless my heart is torn out. If Scott is against peace, he's against me. Besides, I can't possibly love anyone who's pro-war. He's wrong. I'm right.

15

After that, I still had all the parts of my life but they were all bent out of shape; they didn't fit together to make something whole. For instance, I lived on a citrus ranch, but nobody was harvesting and packing oranges there. My dad mostly lay on the sofa, my mother mostly ate, and both of them looked upon me as a mere relic of the daughter they once had. They kept saying, "We're so worried about you," but I felt it was more like disappointed. They wanted their bouncy cheerleader back, along with her star-center boyfriend.

I kept to myself a lot, in my room with the door shut. I told my family I was studying, but mostly I just hung out there thinking. I was going over each moment of my life since the beginning of the school year, trying to figure where I had gone wrong. It was like driving back over the same patch of highway searching for a missed turn. I tried to look into the future without any kind of road map at all, wondering when I was going to stop feeling so lost.

I guess I looked different, too. I mostly wore T-shirts and jeans, and I hardly ever bothered with makeup. I wasn't trying to make myself unattractive, it just didn't seem worth the effort. Most mornings I'd look in the mirror and say to the freshly scrubbed face I found there, "You look fine." Why hadn't I noticed it before? Boys didn't wear makeup, why should girls? Some mornings, though, I took one glance at myself and thought, "Girl, you need help!" A flick of a mascara wand and a swipe of a blush brush made me feel better.

I attended the same high school, I saw the same kids I had known since elementary school, but none of my relationships were the same. I stopped eating lunch at my group's table. I changed the routes I took in the halls to avoid the friends I once had. I switched my seat away from Scott's in Connell's class. I wasn't much into class participation anymore. I just kept quiet and did my work.

I did have one old friend left—Skylar. We still got together for lunch or something every once in a while. She was careful not to mention cheerleading and I was careful not to mention the war, so we didn't have much to talk about. One Saturday we met at Taylor's Hot Dogs for lunch. Skylar seemed more hyper than usual, building pyramids with the little bags of sugar and salt and glancing out into the street as we ate our hot dogs.

Finally she came out with it. "Emily, I was wondering...Um, I was thinking of inviting Scott to the Sadie Hawkins Dance, but only if you don't mind."

My stomach flip-flopped. "Why would I mind? Why would I have any say in it at all?"

"Well, we've all been friends a long time. I wouldn't want to—well, I sort of feel like I'm pulling a Lindsay here."

I thought carefully about what I said next. "Really? It looks to me like you're pulling a Skylar."

That made her blush, but she went on. "Scott's a really great guy. I've liked him a long time, before you even got together with him. Don't get pissed at me or anything but I stood by and watched you take him for granted. You never really seemed to appreciate him much."

After Sadie Hawkins, Scott and Skylar were sort of a couple, so it was no surprise Skylar and I didn't make plans together anymore. At first I was really mad at what she said to me; it kept me awake nights thinking about it. After a while, though, I had to admit to myself she might be right. Maybe I did hold back too much from Scott. But I think it would have been the same with any guy. I just wasn't ready for a serious relationship. I missed Scott; I ached in the hollow spot he left in my heart, but I knew that's the way it had to be.

One afternoon I was walking up our driveway and a basketball hit me square in the stomach. My arms went around it and I held on fast. I thought Scott had suddenly rebounded into my life. I looked up and saw Ryan and some of his friends waiting for me to return the ball. I burst into tears and doubled over. "Ah, barely touched ya," Ryan said, puzzled.

And here was the final bent-out-of-shape thing in my life: the Persian Gulf War. Iraq was getting torn to bits. People were dying there, in Kuwait, and as far away as Israel. Almost everybody around me thought this was the way things were supposed to be. *I* was the crazy person, the idealist, the peace nut—teacher's pet.

Right, I still had Connell. After school I'd swing by her classroom. On my first pass I'd scurry by her open door and dart my eyes inside, sort of like a drive-by shooting. If anyone was with her, I'd go straighten my locker or something, waiting for the coast to clear. One time she and I stayed talking so long the janitor stood at the back of the room clearing his throat, signaling us to leave so he could lock up. Once, I arrived at her classroom to find her gathering up her things.

"Emily, I have to go." She didn't tell me why or where and I shriveled up inside, feeling rejected. I knew I was depending on her too much, but who else did I have?

I started taking my research to her apartment on Saturdays. Sometimes we'd spend whole afternoons piecing together parts of her book and talking. Sometimes she would write while I hung around there doing my homework. Afterward we would have dinner together. Once, we rented the movie *In Country,* about a girl my age whose dad died in the Vietnam War before she was born.

She asks people about him and reads his diary trying to figure out what he was like.

In February my parents let me go away for the weekend with Connell on a research trip to Stanford. When we headed out I suggested we drive north on Highway 63 and catch the Blossom Trail. February is the most beautiful month to be in the San Joaquin Valley, the almond orchards blooming snowstorms and the nectarines and plum trees blushing pastel pink and magenta.

"Oh, we can't make any time on those narrow country roads," said Connell. "Let's hit the freeway and really move."

I nodded in agreement but felt hurt. Her snubbing the natural splendor of my home was like a rejection of me. It wasn't long, though, before we turned off on Highway 152. I felt better winding up Pacheco Pass with its lush green pastures. At Gilroy we merged onto Highway 101, heading into the Bay Area.

At Stanford, Connell strolled through the campus like she belonged there, stretching out her arms and exclaiming, "Well, Emily, what do you think?"

"I love it."

"I, too. Big important brains are at work here. I can feel the thought waves crackling in the air."

"I feel more intelligent just walking through here," I said.

She explained it was actually a rather conservative place. Even so, anti-war posters were plastered everywhere. Looming before us on the quad was a peace symbol two stories high.

Connell put her arm around me and pressed her head against mine. "Well, since your parents won't let you out of the state, this is the place for you. We're going to have to find a way to get you in. I know a few people here, I can try pulling some strings. We'll drive up to Berkeley next. See what you think of the University of California."

"But what about your research work here?"

She held up her small shoulder bag. "Does it look like I've come prepared to work? Haven't you figured it out yet? The research angle was just something to tell your parents. This trip is really about looking at universities for you."

"Really? Why didn't you just say so?"

She shook her head. "Your parents are so overprotective that they probably wouldn't have let you come. This way they think you're slaving away, earning your hourly wage. All parents love to see their children holding down jobs, earning something for themselves, but they hate other adults influencing them. I'll bet if we had told them the truth they would have said *they* could take you to see these schools anytime you wanted, then never get around to it."

I smiled in agreement, but her underestimation of my parents irritated me. Our drive from Palo Alto to Berkeley gave me time to think more about this. Part of me was sure it was unnecessary to lie to my parents. Another part told me her instincts were correct. I guess it was pretty weird for a teen to spend so much time with a teacher. And Mom didn't like Connell from the moment she laid eyes on her in the cereal aisle of the grocery store. Could she be jealous of my affection for Connell? I also wondered if Connell was drawing her conclusions from personal experience. Had she had other young friends like myself whom she'd taken under her wing? That made *me* jealous.

"You're going to love Cal, too," said Connell. "Gorgeous, green rolling hills, stately buildings, the campanile. On clear days you can see all the way across the bay to San Francisco. You know it's the birthplace of the anti–Vietnam War Movement, and—"

"Yes, yes, I've been there."

"You have?"

"Uh-huh. Mom showed me the campus once. She went to Cal for a while. She even protested the war there."

"Really? But she didn't finish?"

"Not there. She graduated from Davis in English lit. Dad has a degree from there in Ag."

"Your parents *both* graduated from college? You never told me that! I just assumed...I mean, so many of your classmates have never had anyone in their families graduate from any college...Well, I guess this little trip of ours isn't so necessary after all."

She was actually mad about it. So I decided to tell her what she wanted to hear. "Oh, but I was only about ten when I visited Cal. College was the farthest thing from my mind then. Besides, it's different being here with you."

The next day, on the drive back to Visalia, we didn't talk much. I spent the time fantasizing about being a student at Stanford.

Nearing Fresno, Connell said abruptly, "Stanford isn't right for you, Emily, nor Cal."

"But just yesterday you said—"

"They would be perfect if they weren't a four-hour drive from your parents. You've just got to convince them to let you go back East, see some of the world, get some perspective. Maybe Vassar—no, too small. Maybe Yale—no, their standards have plummeted. Harvard would be ideal, but it's damn hard to get in. Don't worry, dear, we'll find just the right university for you. I'll see to it."

As time went on Connell became more irritable and tense, lashing out at students, breaking into anti-war tirades. One morning I arrived at school to find her, scissors in hand, snipping yellow ribbons off the chain-link fence, like my mom picking sweet peas. The ribbons were weathered and faded and were hard to replace. Both yellow ribbons and American flags had sold out in our town the first week of the war and had been in short supply ever since.

At one school assembly in which the guest speaker was a local soldier home from the Gulf, Connell stood up in the audience, interrupted him mid-sentence, and began firing questions at him that made him, the US troops, and President Bush appear foolish. Mr. Toledo, the boys' basketball coach, gripped her arm, attempting to guide her back into her seat, but she elbowed him in the ribs. She continued her interrogation until the speaker, red-faced and tongue-tied, left the stage.

In class, Connell's regular lectures disintegrated into philosophical discussions about the dispensability of all war.

Carlos challenged her once by asking, "There's no reason for war—ever? Like there shouldn't have been the Civil War? The great Abraham Lincoln was wrong?"

"Lincoln is considered a great president only because he started a great war. We'd have no Lincoln pennies if he'd done the truly brave thing—negotiated peacefully with the South."

Everyone in class, it seemed, was stealing looks at Darrell Harris—the only African American in our history class. Whenever the topic of slavery came up in front of African Americans, I always felt ashamed of being white. I was especially embarrassed that day because it seemed that Connell was saying that the abolition of slavery wasn't worth fighting for.

"You're saying the South should have been allowed to go on having slavery?" asked another student.

"Absolutely not! It could have been abolished through legislation. Technology would have quickly made slavery economically implausible. The South would have freed the slaves on its own. And, of course, there was the moral issue. Harriet Beecher Stowe, with her *Uncle Tom's Cabin,* rocked the world by detailing the evils of slavery. Given time, slave owners would have eventually been shamed into emancipation.

"But the major cause of the Civil War was that the South seceded!" said Skylar. "You're saying Lincoln was supposed to just let them go start their own country?"

"Not all Southerners were separatists—Lincoln could have worked the sympathy crowd. And there were lots of advantages to being part of the United States. He could have made things pretty tough, forced the South to come crawling back."

"How?"

"Boycotts, for instance. All the cotton was in the South, all the mills were in the North."

"The South could have built its own mills."

"Suppose they did. Suppose the Confederate States of America had survived and was in existence today. What's so bad about two countries instead of one? Have you ever visited Canada? You can hardly tell you've left the United States. A national boundary line is, after all, just a line drawn in the sand. It's not worth what the Civil War cost—six hundred thousand lives."

The class sat silent. Stunned. Mind-boggled. Our teacher had just blasphemed. Abraham Lincoln was wrong? The Civil War was a mistake? I tried to imagine visiting my cousin Lisa in Atlanta and traveling to a different country to get there.

"You believe all that, really, Doc?" asked Carlos.

"I'm not telling you what I believe. I'm giving you something to think about. Do you think there are other solutions besides war?"

After class, Roger Dobbs strode up to Connell, jabbing the air with his finger. "You're crazy and you're dangerous. You don't have any right telling us this crap. You haven't taught any real history in weeks. I'm telling my mother and she's notifying the school board."

"That will be fine, Roger," Connell said calmly. "I'll be happy to explain my teaching strategies to the school board." She turned and began to erase the chalkboard in preparation for her next class.

***

That Saturday I had lunch at Connell's. Dark circles ringed her eyes like she hadn't slept much, and she seemed upset. I tried to keep the conversation going during the meal, but she didn't say much. It made me think she'd rather be alone. As soon as we were done eating, I said I needed to leave and asked her for my research assignment.

"No assignment this week, Emily. Maybe not for a couple of weeks." She took off her glasses, set them on the table, and rubbed her eyes. "I've decided to stop work on the book for a while, take some time to rethink it."

"But why? You said the writing was going so well."

"My editor doesn't believe so. She rejected the sample chapters I sent her."

"But it's so much more interesting than your first book. I can understand it, anyway."

"My editor told me it's too much like my first one. I don't think it is, but she does. In general, books about Vietnam aren't selling much."

"So what? Wouldn't they want to publish a book just because it deserves to be published?"

Connell shook her head. "Publishing is a business; publishers have to make a profit just like everyone else."

"Oh, Connell. I'm really sorry."

"Thanks, Emily. That's more than what I got from *him*. I called *him* to commiserate last night and he just as much as said 'I told you so.'"

My mom sometimes refers to my dad as "him" when he's done something to make her really mad, so I knew Connell meant Stuart.

She stacked the dishes with a loud clatter and shoved away from the table. "I should have known better than to try to get any empathy from *him*. Mr. Hostile Takeover can't possibly understand what I'm trying to do."

I felt a little embarrassed then. This sounded like stuff I wasn't supposed to be hearing, that I couldn't do anything about. I didn't know what to say back.

She walked to the sink and ran water over the dishes. She continued on. "He's always been jealous of me. That's what it is—jealousy—ever since he left the movement and sold out. He's picked at all my writing projects, put me down for the little amount of money they bring in. Just because he doesn't have anything meaningful in his life, he—" Connell stood staring out the window, her shoulders tensed. A look of horror deepened the vertical crease on her brow. "No, no, it can't be!" She turned and dashed out the front door.

I jumped up from the table and went to the window. There was nothing wrong that I could see. Connell was nowhere in sight, and the parking lot was deserted. The day was gray and colorless except for the bright wild mustard shooting up between the walnut trees in the orchard across the highway.

Then I saw Connell run into the street, directly in front of a car. She is going to get hit, I thought. I'm going to watch my teacher die. But the driver slowed down and Connell got safely across.

I ran down the stairs and through the parking lot, then waited for a break in traffic before crossing the highway. When I caught up with Connell, she was kneeling in the mud, crying into her forearms.

"What's wrong?" I asked. "What's wrong?"

"I thought...I thought..." She shuddered deeply. "I didn't have my glasses on. I thought someone...some vicious people...had tied yellow ribbons around every one of these trees."

I thought of that line of poetry—"A host of golden daffodils"—except these were only yellow weeds, extending all the way to the horizon.

16

I was in the cafeteria eating lunch with Elena. We had gotten to know each other well at the peace vigils and through studying AP history and anatomy together.

"So if you don't have the highest grade in the class, and I don't, who does?" she asked.

"No clue." I couldn't think of a single person who was as studious as we were.

Suddenly Connell rushed up to us and tugged on my sleeve. "I need to talk to you in my room, as soon as possible," she whispered in a fervent tone, then walked off.

Elena's eyes were wide behind her little round glasses. "What's that all about?"

I raised my shoulders, then dropped them. I felt embarrassed that Connell hadn't even acknowledged Elena. "I'll tell you when I know myself."

I put away my half-eaten lunch and hurried after Connell.

In her classroom I sat at my assigned desk, my chin in my hand, listening to her rant. Apparently Roger's mom had worked fast.

"The nerve of their damn school board, asking me to resign. They ought to know I don't quit. We'll just have to fight it. I want you to start circulating a petition among the students right away. Get Carlos to help you, and Elena, too."

"I don't know if they will." I figured Carlos wouldn't even sign the petition. In fact, I didn't know a single student besides me and Elena who would want Connell for a teacher if they had a choice.

The vertical crease in her brow deepened. "Maybe a petition isn't the right way to go about this." She snapped her fingers. "A walkout, then."

I imaged myself walking out of school with no one following me. Whoever heard of a walkout of one? I shook my head. "It's against school rules. I'd get suspended."

"So what? The important thing is to stand up for what you believe in."

I spoke up, even though I knew she wouldn't like it. "I don't think it would be right to have a suspension on my records."

"They can't suspended all my students."

"But what if not too many of them will walk out? These are some of the best kids in the school—they don't want suspensions on their records either. You've made a lot of people angry, taking down those yellow ribbons, insulting that guest speaker."

"Which guest—oh, him. He was trying to indoctrinate you students with a lot of propaganda."

"He was a guest speaker at a school assembly."

Connell waved away my comment. "An inappropriate choice. I tried to warn Principal Cisneros about him."

"Emily, what is going on here? Why are you, of all people, siding against me?"

"I'm not! Of course I don't want to lose you for a teacher. I feel terrible about this. But I'm just one kid. I don't know how I can help you."

"I need this job!" She began to search for a tissue in her purse.

"Have you talked to your husband about this?"

"Stuart wants a separation. Oh, I know you think we're always separated. I mean a divorce. He's met someone." She blew her nose and dabbed at her eyes.

"Oh, Connell! Why didn't you tell me? I'm so sorry!"

"It's just one more thing."

"You really want to keep teaching here?"

"Of course. Where else would I go?"

"Maybe if you apologized to the board and tried to change their minds. You could promise to stick to the subject matter."

"Subject matter! I have been covering the subject matter. It's my interpretation that the school board objects to."

"It's more than that." I began to quake inside. It wasn't my place to criticize her teaching, but if she heard it from me, I thought it might help. "Your teaching has changed. *You* have. After the war started you just...I'm sorry, Connell. I don't want you to think...Well, actually, you upset your students, intimidate them. It's very scary to think of a country in existence today called the Confederate States of America."

"What? Oh, that. It was just a harmless little 'what if' to get you thinking. Teachers are supposed to encourage thought among students, are they not?" Her tone became louder, sharper. "That isn't against the school board, is it? My God, I don't believe this. You're against me, too."

"Connell, I'm not against you. I'm just trying to help you see—"

"Help me? You're not going to help me at all, are you? After all I've done for you, you can't be bothered to even—oh, hell, forget it. What am I doing here confiding in a cheerleader?"

As her voice got louder, mine got quieter. I was just as hurt and angry as she was, but it gave me strength to stay in control. "I'm not a cheerleader anymore. Remember? I gave that up for you."

"For me? What have I got to do with it? You don't have the moral conscience to find the whole ritual repulsive?"

"I guess I don't." I walked out of Connell's classroom. Something snapped inside me. Something that felt like chains. I broke into a run, feeling as free as I had at age ten—no, sixteen. I felt like I could act my age again. Lindsay! Crazy, wild, irresponsible Lindsay, my childhood friend. I needed to find her right away.

I searched the cafeteria, the quad, the locker room. I swung around a corner and nearly bumped into Carlos.

"Where is she?"

He tilted his head back toward the women's room.

"Thanks." I started to walk around him, but he stepped in front of me.

"Hold on, Emily, what's the rush? We haven't seen much of you these days."

I didn't answer. I didn't know what to say.

His long arms stretched around me, his palms slapped against the wall on either side, trapping me. I looked into his wide brown eyes and saw that he wasn't playing. He was looking deeply into me like he wanted something, but I didn't understand what it was. I pushed one of his arms down and was surprised he didn't resist.

"Emily, how come you don't talk to your friends anymore?"

I averted my eyes. If this was a staring match, he'd won. Is that how my friends saw it, really? I thought they had alienated me. Maybe I had ostracized myself. For what? To hang out with a teacher?

Carlos pushed away from the wall. "We miss you, Emily."

"Thanks. I miss you guys, too. I didn't realize how much until—oh, Carlos, so much has happened. I'm sort of mixed up right now."

"The Doc's in trouble, isn't she?"

"What would you care?"

Carlos shrugged. "I don't agree with her politics, but she's still the best teacher I ever had."

I placed my hands on my hips and narrowed my eyes. "Oh, right. You're not one of the kids that complained about her? I guess you're used to getting Ds."

An illuminated look swept over his face, then vanished so fast I would have missed it if I'd blinked. "One day last semester you said you got a D, but that isn't right, is it?"

Carlos smirked. "I got a reputation to keep up. Wouldn't want the guys to think I was a schoolboy."

"It's you, then. Elena and I were wondering today who could possibly have the highest grade in the class. How did you manage that?"

"I don't know. I guess Doc likes the way I answer her essay questions."

"You would have had to do all the required reading."

He shrugged. "It was pretty interesting, most of the time."

I remember Carlos in elementary school, spending more time standing out in the hall than inside the classroom. Once in fourth grade we had a substitute and he spent the whole day camped out under his desk. Our sixth-grade teacher, Mrs. Silverman, screamed at him, "You are capable of doing better work." Could it be that Connell was the first teacher who had ever challenged him?

"You're right," I said. "Dr. McKenzie is in trouble. It's the school board. They want her to resign."

"That sucks. What can we do about it?"

It was my turn to shrug. I walked into the bathroom. Lindsay was in there alone, leaning into the mirror, her pretty lips pressed out in a self-absorbed pout as she tried to cover a pimple on her chin. On the mirror ledge, lined up like artillery, were Clearasil, liquid foundation, face powder, stick concealer, and blush. No matter what she used, the zit still showed, pink and puffy. I truly wished she wasn't having such a tough time of it. No one is perfect, but that doesn't mean every kid isn't thrown into a panic at the realization of a mere blemish. Lindsay was no longer the close childhood friend she once was, but she wasn't my nemesis either. She was trying to make the best of what she had, just like me.

Her eyes met mine in the mirror and she whirled around, looking stricken, as if I had caught her at something I'd use against her.

I looked down at her ankle. The bruises had faded to a brownish-green and her foot was slightly swollen. When I saw her around school, she still limped. She had suffered a lot because of my negligence, and only now did I feel any sympathy or remorse. "Hey, Lindsay, I'm sorry about what happened."

"Thanks, Emily, even though you're, like, way late."

"Oh, but I'm not. I'm right on time. I mean, the second I felt sorry I came looking for you. Sorry it took me so long."

"Oh, you're not just saying it! You're really *sorry* sorry?"

I laughed. We hugged. Lindsay shouted "Waaugh!" right into my ear.

***

Each afternoon that week I went straight home from school and up to my room. One day on my way upstairs I noticed Daddy, as usual, lying on the sofa staring up at the ceiling. It struck me then that he wasn't just lying there—he was thinking things through, just like me. It was taking him a lot of time to work out his problems, too, even though they were far different from the kind I was having.

I tried to forgive Connell for some of the hurtful things she had said to me, for trying to manipulate me, for ruining my life. I told myself it wasn't her fault I had fallen under her spell. I thought about all the actions I had taken over the last several months, all the decisions I had made. For each one I asked myself, Did I do this thing for Connell or for myself?

Her. No, her *and* me.

No, her. No, me.

Me.

Her.

Her—no, me.

Me.

***

It seemed for a while that Connell had struck a deal with the school board. All that week in her lectures she kept strictly to the text, a paragraph-by-paragraph synopsis of Ulysses S. Grant's eight-year administration. She delivered his account in a quiet monotone, barely audible above the hum of classroom chatter. She looked straight ahead, her shining eyes focused over our heads, like an amateur actor just trying to get through a miserable performance.

On Friday, five minutes before the bell, Connell knocked on her desk for our attention and spoke loudly and firmly, like her old self. "Class, I have an announcement. This is my last day with you."

So she hadn't tried to appease the board; she had merely done what was necessary to get through the week. I was struck with a deep sadness. I no longer wanted to be her friend, her confidante, but I badly wanted to continue being her student.

"I want to say goodbye." She ignored the rising hum and some low-key cheers. "I want you all to know I have tried..." She looked directly at me and I averted my eyes. "I have tried to give you a different perspective, a different viewpoint, a nonconventional way of thinking about history. My choices were not popular. I have upset some of you and your parents and the school board. Nonetheless, I tried to incite your thought process, get you to think for yourselves." She glanced at Carlos, at Elena, and again at me. "In some instances, I believe I have accomplished this."

Several seconds of silence passed. Roger Dobbs belched loudly. The class cracked up. The bell rang. We all filed out.

After school, on my first swipe past Connell's opened classroom door I found her bent over boxes and books on her desk, only the crown of her honey head visible.

On my second pass, I stood in the door, my heart thudding. She looked up, her eyes registering only that she had felt someone's presence. My intention was to wait until her eyes responded to mine. But, lacking the nerve, I bolted.

17

Most of Desert Storm took place in the air, but, to free Kuwait, the allied forces had to eventually battle on the ground. This is what we all feared. It was one thing to shoot at the Iraqis from the air, like ducks in a barrel; it was another to meet them on desert sand, face to face.

The allied ground offensive began on February 23, and in a hundred hours it was over. Sitting in front of the TV, popcorn and sodas in hand, my family and I watched column after column of Iraqi soldiers rise out of foxholes in the sand, their bare fingertips appearing first, and then their haggard faces and tattered uniforms. They threw down their guns, sunk to their knees, and begged for mercy and food. They seemed to look upon their enemies almost as their liberators. Many had been holed up in the desert for seven months, and apparently Hussein had not had the provisions to feed them. Some Iraqi soldiers reported subsisting on a spoonful of rice a day. The surrendered Iraqi soldiers trekked across the desert with their captors, like a row of two hundred thousand dominoes, all falling after one gentle shove. It was all so easy, I believe even General Schwarzkopf looked stunned.

Next on TV came scenes of the devastation Hussein left behind in Kuwait. Worst of all, knowing defeat was near, the Iraqis had set fire to one hundred Kuwaiti oil wells. Finally, we watched a brigade of Kuwaiti soldiers reclaim Kuwait City. They stood on their tanks, laughing and waving their flag. They jumped down and began dancing in the streets. Tears welled in my eyes: the war was over.

***

On the first Sunday in March, some of us who had stood together for peace those many weeks assembled in Mooney Grove to pay our last respects to one hundred and fifty members of the allied forces and an estimated one hundred thousand Iraqi soldiers and civilians who had lost their lives in the Persian Gulf War.

The day was clear and cool. A bitter wind whipped around us and dust devils whirled at our ankles. We stood in an informal circle, waiting to begin, some of us talking, musicians tuning guitars. We'd put a notice in the *Times-Delta* about our memorial service, careful not to mention that five-letter word that seemed like a four-letter word to most citizens in Tulare County. We wanted everyone, pro-war and anti-war, to come together in our final meeting.

A few last cars drove up to our congregation and parked. One was Scott's Mustang. He got out and so did his Uncle Gary, his head bent, his silver-blonde ponytail reflecting the sunlight. I waved to them, trying to catch their attention, but they didn't see me. Scott approached a gray-bearded man in a red beret and asked if this was the memorial service.

The man nodded. "This is the place."

"My uncle and I would like to honor the US troops who laid down their lives for freedom," Scott said.

"Come join us then," said the man. "We're only going to sing a few songs, speak if we're moved."

Scott led Gary to the circle. Several men unfolded an American flag and held it up. Several others unfurled a three-foot banner reading "Tulare County Peace Committee." A look of disgust crossed Scott's face. He grabbed his uncle's sleeve and pulled. Gary seemed reluctant to move and they argued in hushed voices as Scott pointed to the banner.

"Fine!" he burst out. "Find your own ride home."

Gary stopped arguing, his eyes following Scott to his car.

I hurried up to them. "Hi, you guys."

"Hi, Emily." Scott pulled the bill of his cap farther down on his face and looked away. It was hard to tell what he felt for me, if he felt anything at all.

"I kind of overheard you guys. I can take Gary home if you don't want to stay, Scott."

"Why thank you, Emily. I'd sure appreciate it."

Without a word, Scott got into his car and backed out. When would he stop taking sides, I wondered, if he couldn't stop it now? I felt sorry for him. Watching him ride off, I thought of a helium balloon I had let fly away. The release was uplifting, but I also felt sadness in the loss. In my heart I let go of Scott that day. In the scrapbook of my mind I placed a picture of a tall, beautiful boy reaching high for an orange on the coldest night of my life.

"Goodbye, Scottie," I yelled into the roar of his retreating car. Goodbye, my love.

In the circle of mourners I held hands with the old man in the red beret on one side of me and Gary on the other. Together we sang "Let there be peace on earth, and let it begin with me."

Yes, I take personal responsibility. Let it begin with me.

***

The war ended but the killing continued. Throughout March and April, horror stories poured out of Iraq. Factions within the country—the Shi'ite Muslims in the south and the Kurds in the north—thought this was a good time to rise up against Hussein. The rebels were ruthlessly put down. Iraqi soldiers opened fire on Shi'ite Muslim schoolchildren. The Kurds were napalmed. They fled to the mountains, many only to die of starvation, exposure, and disease. The American military finally showed up to protect the refugees, but by then it was too late for many of them. Another estimated one hundred thousand Iraqis lost their lives.

I missed Connell. I wanted to commiserate with her. Our new history teacher, Mr. Speers, a young man fresh out of college, didn't talk current events in his class. He stuck to the text, sometimes reading passages aloud, as if he had been duly warned by the fate of his predecessor.

I turned to Mom. "Why do the Kurds have to suffer so much? I've been racking my brain trying to figure what could have been done differently to save them."

"Certainly you would not have been in favor of prolonging the war," said Mom.

"No. It wouldn't make sense for Americans to kill a bunch of Iraqis in cold blood only to prevent them from killing their own people in cold blood. Besides, once Kuwait was free, what would be our reason? Hussein has the excuse that he's putting down a rebellion."

Mom nodded. "And our country has faced situations like this before, in which the military goes in, helps to overthrow the existing government, and sets up one of their own choosing, but it never works out. It only leads to more bloodshed."

"Still, Bush encouraged the Kurds to overthrow Hussein. I can see where they took that to mean he would help them. It's like he set them up to be slaughtered. I feel the US is indirectly responsible for this. We had no business in the Middle East in the first place."

"We freed Kuwait," Mom said. "We got Hussein to toe the line."

"And he's more powerful than ever. And more cruel. Too bad the Kurds don't have a couple hundred oil wells to call their own. Bush would have helped them then."

"Oh, Emmie! I hate to see you so cynical about your own country."

I raised my arms and let them slap against my sides. "I hate this war! The whole thing was so stupid!"

At the end of April, Kurdish leader Jalal Talabani came down from the mountains to Baghdad. Hussein kissed his cheek and after that there was some kind of peace in Iraq—along with terrorism and oppression.

I suppose after that the Iraqis started picking up the pieces, trying to get their lives back to normal. The same thing went on in the San Joaquin Valley. One day my dad got off the sofa, went out to the groves, and discovered trees that he thought had died in the freeze belatedly sprouting new growth.

Another morning I was awakened by what sounded like a wild boar snorting through the groves. I bounded to my window, looked down, and spotted my mom, jogging in her navy sweats, her wide bubble butt bouncing along like an oversized beach ball. She continued jogging every morning through spring and summer. I never heard her mention the word "diet," but Hershey's Kisses disappeared from our house, and salad and broiled fish and chicken appeared on our dinner table. The twenty-plus pounds she gained over the winter melted away.

Over the summer, I took a volunteer job teaching illiterate adults how to read. It felt good to do something useful that didn't have anything to do with world peace. It helped me gain perspective. I soon reached the point where I could hold my tongue and control my speeding pulse when someone happened to mention what a great job Bush had done in the Persian Gulf War. I allowed people the right to their own opinions. I stopped making enemies of anyone who did not share my political outlook.

I started dating Alfred Mendel, the son of a friend of my parents, home from college for the summer. He's a music major at USC—a bassoonist whose goal is to get a position in a good European orchestra. I admitted on our first date that I didn't remember what a bassoon sounded like. Alfred, who has a blonde beard and a stocky build, laughed and said, "It's the grandfather in *Peter and the Wolf*," and right away I did know. Sparks don't especially fly between us—he doesn't want a serious relationship any more than I do—but he's funny and intelligent and he takes me to lots of concerts of classical music. I still don't know much about it, a lot of it seems too slow and boring, but one time when we were listening to an orchestra play something by this composer I'd never heard of—Mahler—one part of the music made me sit straight up in my seat and after a few moments I had to remind myself to start breathing again.

Alfred has no feelings about the war one way or the other. He says a practice room is kind of a world of its own and it's hard to keep track of what's going on outside of it. I think a lot of people live like this, in their own little rooms, not because they are concentrating on anything hard like bassoon playing, but because they are so wound up in their busy personal lives. I was like that before I met Connell, before the Big Freeze of '90, before the Persian Gulf War. Experiencing these things made me look beyond my next back flip in cheerleading or the next A on a history test. They cracked the world wide open for me.

***

One evening just last week, after Alfred went back to Los Angeles to begin the school year, Mom and I sat out on the patio together. A soft gray darkness settled over the Sierra, the orange trees were rustling silhouettes, and the stars were poking out all over the place, like pinholes in black construction paper. In my heart I felt a deep contentment, layered over by a heavy longing. I sighed deeply.

"He'll be back, honey, on weekends."

"I was thinking of *her*."

"Oh." My mom shifted in her chaise lounge.

"I wonder about her, where she is, what's she doing, how she's doing."

My mom turned to me, her features barely visible in the gloaming. It was hard to know what she was feeling. "You do that a lot, don't you? Daydream about your Dr. Connell McKenzie."

"My mind keeps playing back the same old scenes. I have imaginary conversations with her all the time. Sometimes I fantasize attending a university and she's my teacher again, or she's not my teacher, just my friend. Sometimes I catch myself talking and acting a way that isn't the real me but the way I think she would want me to be, and it makes me mad at myself. I keep hoping to wake up some morning and realize she's nothing to me, a mere distant memory."

"Maybe it'll never come to that."

"Oh, Mom, it just has to!"

"I have a Dr. McKenzie, too. Her name is Mrs. Silverthorne. I used to baby-sit for her when I was about your age. She was an Avon lady."

"An Avon lady?" I was sure my mom was off on a tangent that had nothing to do with what I wanted to talk about.

"She was recently divorced—her husband had left her for a much younger woman—and she was determined to make a new glamorous life for herself. She attended courses in fashion design at the local community college and sold Avon for a little income. The trouble was she couldn't quite fit her three kids into her new life. During the summer months I'd sometimes baby-sit for her twenty to forty hours per week."

"So?"

"Women didn't leave their kids much in those days; they were tied to the home. It struck me that it was a brave thing to do—something my mother and the other women in the neighborhood didn't approve of." Mom paused. I thought that was the end of the saga, and we sat together enjoying the quiet darkness for a while.

Then she continued. "She would say, 'Now, Bonita, you know your name means "beautiful" in Spanish.' Actually it's more like 'pretty,' but Mrs. Silverthorne insisted 'beautiful.' And she'd say, 'Well, you certainly don't act like you know it. Here, let me make you over.' She made me over once a week. And afterward, I *did* feel beautiful, that is, until I walked into my own house and my mother said, 'Go wash your face! You look cheap!'

"Mrs. Silverthorne also gave me my sex education. We would have wonderful discussions that would leave me breathless. She was seeing a lifeguard, Derek, at the community pool, a college boy about ten years younger than she—I guess there was a little of her showing her ex-husband. All the girls at the pool my age would swoon over Derek's big, bronze muscles, giggle, and flirt with him, but we knew we were just kids to him and Mrs. Silverthorne was the real thing. She would come home and tell me all about it. Once she gripped my arm, leaned toward me, and said, 'Oh, Bonita, don't get married young! Have something of your own first.' And you know, Emmie, I'm certain she wasn't talking about sex."

"Where is she now?'

"Oh, who knows? She skipped town one night, her kids in tow, owing me $47.50. At fifty cents an hour that was a lot of money."

"Were you mad?"

"And hurt. Worse, I felt betrayed. But it wasn't personal. She left owing the paperboy, the milkman, and she was behind in her rent."

"Do you wish you could find out what happened to her?"

"Sort of. Not really. She'd be in her sixties now. She wouldn't be my Mrs. Silverthorne, the one stuck in my brain."

"And you still think about her, after all this time?"

"And talk to her in my mind. Some times more than others. I actually did a lot of explaining to her this winter, why I had to eat so much candy, why my husband couldn't get off the sofa, how worried I was about you after you quit cheerleading."

"I don't believe it, Mom. How she could be such an influence and you never mentioned her to me."

"Ah, Emmie-Em, she's not a big part of my life. She's not any part at all. She exists only inside of me."

"Why do you think she made such an impression on you?"

I watched the silhouette of my mother's head turning slowly from side to side. "I've asked myself that a hundred times and I still don't know. Mostly, I think, it was just the thrill of knowing her. She made me feel such strong feelings."

The next day I got Connell's letter.

18

So here I am, holding Connell's letter, writing back to her in my mind. I tell her I'm sitting alone in the bleachers at Sunkist Stadium on a blistering, white-bright, late-August morning, waiting for cheerleading tryouts to start. Yep, Connell, I'm going back to the squad if Coach Metz and the girls will have me. It was a big mistake to quit last year. It hurt me a lot; how much I didn't know until later. Cheerleading is my sport and I love it. I quit it for all the wrong reasons: because of my pride, because I thought it was what you wanted me to do, and because I thought what you wanted for me was what I wanted for myself.

Sitting here in this familiar place I feel changed from one year ago. I feel wiser, Connell. I feel stronger, more capable, less gullible. I don't think I'll ever be so easily influenced by anyone. Somehow, too, I feel more weighed down. I'm sobered by how big a place the world is and by how badly things can go wrong.

I'll always be a pacifist, Connell. I now have a direction in my life. In college I want to major in political science. I'd like to be an ambassador or something. I want to work to connect the world together. Peace is possible, Connell. I have to go on believing that.

A hot breeze causes her letter to flutter. In it she writes that she is working on her book again—a university press might want to publish it. She has a one-year teaching position at a small liberal arts college, close enough to Boston so she can spend weekends with Stuart (they are working at a reconciliation). I'm glad for Connell. She seems to be back on track, just like I am. Life really does go on.

My mom told me she thinks things like *How do you like the carpeting in the family room, Mrs. Silverthorne? It's a little too light for such a high-traffic area, but we'll see; the kids are getting older and don't track in as much. Isn't Ryan tall for his age, Mrs. Silverthorne? And my Emmie is growing into a wonderful young woman. And my Sam, it's true, he's aged this year—more gray at the temples, deeper creases around the eyes. That freeze knocked us for a loop, Mrs. Silverthorne, but we're back on our feet. We'll have a modest crop of valencias. We'll go marketing to Montreal and New York and Seattle. And yes, Mrs. Silverthorne, by then I'll be able to fit into all my beautiful clothes.*

I fold Connell's letter and shove it deep into my pocket, wondering if I'll ever answer it. It hardly seems to matter. Like Mrs. Silverthorne in my mom, Connell is in me. Some people just stick with you. They grab a hold of a corner of your brain and hang on for life. I said in the beginning of this story that a person, Dr. Connell McKenzie, happened to me. That's the best way I can explain it.

I see Skylar at the gate now. Donna is right behind her and Sharon and Lindsay. I wave, let out a joyous whoop, and run to greet my team.

Great Valley Books is an imprint of Heyday Books, a nonprofit publishing company based in Berkeley, California. Created in 2002 with a grant from the James Irvine Foundation and with the support of the Great Valley Center (Modesto, California), the Great Valley series strives to publish, promote, and develop a deep appreciation of various aspects of the region's unique history and culture. We are grateful to James McClatchy for his support of this volume.